The Devil's Teacup

and Other Ghost Stories

BIBHUTIBHUSHAN BANDYOPADHYAY

Translated by **PRASUN ROY**

FiNGERPRINT!

Published by

FiNGERPRINT!

An imprint of Prakash Books India Pvt. Ltd

113/A, Darya Ganj,
New Delhi-110 002
Email: info@prakashbooks.com/sales@prakashbooks.com

 Fingerprint Publishing
 @FingerprintP
 @fingerprintpublishingbooks
www.fingerprintpublishing.com

ISBN: 978 93 5856 617 8

Dedication

To my beautiful children, Ekalavya and Ekantika.

Acknowledgments

A big thank you to everyone who has been beside me throughout my journey, especially my family, who have been my constant support system. Without your support and inspiration, I am always incomplete.

A special thanks to the team at The Book Bakers, one of the leading literary agencies in the country today, for believing in my work, shaping my literary journey over the years and motivating me to experiment with different literary styles. My literary agent, Suhail Mathur, has consistently invested faith in my writing, especially this manuscript. I feel fortunate to be associated with him and his team. Suhail has been a friend, a brother, and a guide to me.

I sincerely thank my dynamic publisher, Fingerprint Publishing, for their undeterred faith in this book. I want to thank Shantanu Duttagupta, executive publisher of Fingerprint Publishing. His expert advice has greatly enriched this book.

The Devil's Teacup and Other Ghost Stories is my honest effort to translate 13 timeless stories of

Bibhutibhushan Bandyopadhyay that can take the readers on a rollercoaster ride beyond the barriers of time and horror. It is an endeavor that provides the readers with a golden opportunity to enjoy these classic treasures of Bengali literature. I sincerely hope everybody will enjoy reading this book as much as I have enjoyed translating it.

CONTENTS

The Phantom Bed

That evening, I met Satish. Rather, I must say that I bumped into Satish after a long time. In the crowded and busy footpath of Bentick Street, he was hurrying down, as he struggled to push his way forward. The street was cramped as every office-goer was rushing to head home. That evening, I was walking down the road wearily, yet cautiously, amid that craze. I was tired after a long day at the office. Then suddenly, I saw Satish at a distance.

With a rush of adrenaline, I clutched his shirt and exclaimed, "Satish, it's you, my buddy! Where are you going in such a hurry?"

An equally startled Satish replied in a scream of joy, "It's you, Khagen! By God! I was looking for you."

I said angrily, "Don't you lie. You passed me in such great haste! You wouldn't have even noticed me if I hadn't called you."

"Sorry, my friend, but I am very busy," responded Satish, as his face turned red with awkwardness.

I smiled and added, "That is totally evident, my dear. Now tell me, where are you going?"

He felt relieved and said vigorously, "You must come with me! Yes, let's go. It's not very far from here. I will tell you everything as we go."

"That is outrageous!" I tried to revolt meekly.

"I shall not accept your 'No' as a reply. Now come with me, or else I shall drag you along. Quick, we cannot lose a single moment," said Satish stubbornly.

Satish, my buddy, the good old fellow, was like this from his childhood. I had known him since we were kids. He always acted as per his own words and I never—willingly or unwillingly—tried to resist him. Being stronger physically, he always succeeded in accomplishing his demands and desires. Despite everything, he was my dearest friend. Therefore, I consented and went ahead with him toward the mysterious destination. Honestly, I couldn't refuse my friend, especially when I met him after such a long time.

His destination wasn't that far. As we went, he revealed his intentions in brief. That morning, there was a peculiar advertisement in the newspaper. Satish took out a piece of paper, handed it over to me and said, "Here, read this."

An exceptionally modern and equally mysterious Chinese bedstead is available to be sold off to the highest bidder. This exclusive furniture is incomparable! This is a golden opportunity to own such a masterpiece and it would be imprudent to miss it.

2 | 3 . . . . Street.

"Alright," I replied after reading the excerpt, "but what is the meaning of the word 'mysterious' in this?"

"That is why I am curious," Satish replied fervently, "I am yet to discover any clue about it."

Satish and I were walking down the footpath, and as we spoke, his eyes were scanning the names of the streets. Then, he stopped abruptly near a lane and said with a brisk jump of joy, "Finally, we found it!"

In the dim light of the setting sun, the sight of that lane brought a cascade of shivers down my spine. The evening seemed to be the shroud of the devil's workshop as it uncovered the path toward the mysterious bedstead somewhere within that dingy and equally shadowy neighborhood.

In that sudden rush of fear, I clutched Satish's hand firmly and begged, "Satish, let's not waste our time on that weird bed. Let us go back quickly. I am not getting a very good vibe about this."

He blurted in anger while he shook my shoulders with both his hands, "You coward! After coming this far, I will not go back! Come with me."

On the right side of the lane's entrance, a huge neem tree stood with its branches stretched like the arms of a monstrous ghost. On the other side, an overfull dustbin ejected an intolerable stench into the air and almost choked our breath. I took out my handkerchief, held it over my nose and mouth, and quickly headed inside the lane with Satish.

A gust of chilly wind blew in from the south and lashed upon our skin. As we shivered in that eerie cold breath of an invisible phantom, a few vampire bats flew past above our heads. The flapping sounds of their wings were equally uncanny. Two mongrels stood at a distance and barked at us, voicing their distant protest. Devoid of any human presence, the dark lane grew eerier with every passing moment. As we walked, I noticed a decrepit signboard of a Chinese doctor's clinic. Even though the place was closed, the ramshackled painting of a skeleton (atop the signboard) stared at us ruthlessly. From somewhere close, the sound of a piano floated in the air and made the background even more spooky.

Maybe it was our subconscious fear that was playing games, but in that secluded lane, it did give a hair-raising sensation.

Soon, we reached our destination. To be honest, I had never seen a house like that before. It was a dilapidated structure where the ruined brick walls were like the broken teeth of a gaping face whose emaciated body had endured the test of time for centuries, perhaps, from the time of Nawab Alivardi Khan.[1]

Through a crumbling door, we carefully entered and went inside cautiously. However, as we went in, the entire ambience seemed magically distinctive from what it was outside! Both Satish and I were amazed to see a huge crowd. It was astonishing to see such an enormous gathering inside the house . . . a distinct contrast to the uninhabited street outside. The air within carried a shivering eeriness. Each of their faces carried an uncanny yet unknown thrill while a grinding silence prevailed in every direction.

An hour later, a very old and fat Chinese man appeared and guided us inside. This man, too, had a strange appearance. His head was completely bald, and two of his teeth were made of gold! There was a tattoo of a dagger on his left arm that made him appear mysterious. The entire house was like a fortified maze, and we finally reached the room where the enigmatic bedstead was kept.

At first sight, we both understood that it was indeed something invaluable. What a bed it was! I had never seen such a thing in my whole life. It was truly immaculate and neither before nor after that, I had seen such a piece of Chinese furniture. The brilliant sculpturing and flawless architecture in each and every engraving were undeniably beyond all appreciation. On one side, there was the sculpture of a meditating Buddha with a serenely beautiful countenance. The bedstead was not very big; it was decent enough to accommodate two people. However, with a marvelous architectural

---

[1] Alivardi Khan was the Nawab of Bengal from 1740 to 1756.

genius, it could be unfolded, if necessary, to accommodate ten individuals comfortably. Both Satish and I stood spellbound as we kept staring at the incredible bed.

As the auction started, every prospective buyer started to place their bids vigorously. Their eyes glinted with a deep desire to own the masterpiece. The price, too, started to rise in leaps and bounds. Lastly, Satish emerged victorious in that battle—he won it with a prize worth fifteen hundred rupees!

Satish and I reached his home with the bed around ten o' clock at night. Whoever saw it, couldn't help but say, "It really is fantastic."

After dinner, I got up to return home. With a contented smile on his lips, Satish said, "Come soon. It is a heartfelt invitation from me and my bed."

*

However, before I could honor the open invitation, Satish himself came to visit me . . . the next morning!

I was absolutely startled to see Satish in such a distraught state. His hair was in a mess. His face was dry and pale while his eyes were entirely red. It was evident that due to some unforeseen anxiety or trepidation, Satish had not slept even for a minute throughout the entire night.

I asked him worriedly, "What happened?"

"Danger! Calamity! A catastrophe has befallen," he screamed out tensely.

"What danger? What catastrophe? Please explain everything," I exclaimed.

"That . . . that bed!" he cried frantically.

"I was certain that something unusual would happen inevitably. You yourself have invited a predator inside the house! Satish, after all, that is a mysterious bed, didn't I warn you?" I asked angrily.

With a distressed face, Satish revealed the tale of his previous night's ordeal in detail. The poor man had spent a sleepless night in sheer terror. He was lying on his new prized bed, when, at around midnight, he felt as if somebody was shaking the bed violently. When he switched on the lights, surprisingly, everything seemed normal. He looked around a bit, switched off the lights, and went to bed again. After some time, his sleep was interrupted by another sudden jolt, and the echoes of an appalling voice filled the entire room. Then, the phantom bed automatically began to bang against the wall while Satish shuddered and crouched helplessly upon it. With all his courage, Satish again managed to turn the lights on, but everything became still almost immediately. A traumatized Satish then kept the lights on and tried to close his eyes in the hope of some sleep, but destiny had other plans. The heartbreaking cries of an eerie feminine voice froze his blood with fear. In the absence of any other human inside the room, the creepy sobs pierced through his heart. It seemed as though a ghost was sitting by the bedside, weeping in a creepy and colossal sorrow.

I yelled, "I had warned you from the start. I told you not to buy that mysterious bed. But you were too stubborn. And now, you are facing the consequences."

"Listen to me Khagen," responded Satish helplessly, "I may not be able to make you understand . . . but an irresistible attachment binds me with that horrific bed. Even if I try, I wouldn't be able to detach myself from it. Khagen, my pal . . . I just cannot stay away from that bed!"

"Then go and be damned with your phantom bed!" I retorted angrily. The entire episode was too irritating, and I felt angry with Satish for his foolish intoxication toward an innate piece of furniture.

"Khagen!" added Satish with a pale face, "Khagen, I need your help."

I looked at him and asked crossly, "My help? How can I help you?"

"Yes. Tonight, you must stay with me in my house, in the same room where that bed is," said Satish earnestly. "You must watch that wretched bed throughout the night and find out the reason behind whatever happened. Only you can help me! Please, I really need your support. Stay awake and see what that thing does! Khagen, I cannot abandon that bed, so please help me!"

I was spellbound for a moment and replied, "But, I have office tomorrow. How can I stay awake all night?"

Satish laughed sardonically and said, "Tomorrow is a Sunday!"

*

Despite all my stubbornness and anger, Satish was a dear friend. I couldn't refuse his heartfelt request. At last, I agreed. That evening, I reached his house and saw that he was waiting for me. As I entered, he jumped with joy and screamed, "Welcome! Welcome, my buddy. I knew you would come."

I sat down on the sofa in the living room and asked, "Did anything happen again?"

Satish grinned and replied, "None! As expected, the mysterious bed won't cause any trouble during the day."

Satish's mother came with an agitated countenance and said to me, "Khagen, I am really worried. What is happening with your friend? I have been pleading with Satish to discard that wretched bed and sell it off at the earliest, but he has become so hard-headed! He is not paying any heed to my words. Son, I am very worried. Please do something to make him understand. That cursed thing must be cast off immediately."

Satish revolted, "Maa, what are you saying? Gripped by an irrational fear, how can I discard a bed worth fifteen hundred rupees?"

After dinner, the two of us went upstairs and entered Satish's room where he had kept the mysterious bed. I had a book with me while Satish held a book on health and hygiene. As we reclined upon the bed, I opened my book, but was unable to read even a page. My eyes kept meandering across the room while my ears remained on high alert in the hope of hearing some eerie noises. Deep within, I was scared and apprehensive about what was about to happen. My heart was palpitating with fear, thinking that at any moment some evil entity would grip our throats with its malicious hands!

We planned to take turns to stay awake and keep watch while the other would take some sleep. That would enable us to keep a complete record of anything unusual that might happen. First, it was Satish's turn to rest while I stayed awake.

Suddenly, the sound of a distant clock floated in as a herald . . . *It is already ten o' clock!*

The sound reverberated in my ears and all of a sudden, I distinctly felt that somebody was pacing around on the adjoining veranda. I clearly heard every footstep of that unearthly and invisible creature. The shudders raised every hair on my body.

Then, with a jolt of an unknown force, the open window banged and shut involuntarily! Before I could react, I felt as if I had been projected up in the air by some ghastly supernatural force. All my consciousness became numb, and I was in an absolute state of terrified trauma. Was I alive, or was I dead already? I didn't have any answers. I was too shocked to think. My brain was in a state of comatoseness, and my whole body was trembling with the utmost dread.

I shrieked aloud, "Satish! Satish, what is happening?"

Satish stumbled up upon the bed and shouted, "What? What happened? What is going on?"

My trance was unbroken. My gaping mouth was still devoid of any sound. Satish held my shoulders and shook me heavily. He again shouted, "Khagen! Khagen, look at me. What is wrong?"

As my cognizance slowly returned, I wiped away the drops of perspiration from my forehead and said softly in a trembling voice, "Oh! It was ghastly. I was at the pinnacle of something too horrific. I was in a complete state of shock."

He said, "Oh God. Your pitiable state is more than visible. Khagen, you don't have to stay awake. Now, sleep for some time. I will stay awake while you take some rest."

"No," I replied, "I don't want to sleep anymore. Well, honestly, I don't think I would be able to sleep any further tonight."

Satish grinned and added, "Khagen, you are really a coward!"

Hence, both Satish and I, the two friends who were epitomes of cowardliness that night, sat upon the uncanny bed and silently waited for the nightly hours to pass. I stared at the open window and looked outside at the slice of open sky that was still studded with twinkling stars. In a poetic mood, it seemed as though the distant heavenly objects were smirking at us.

The two of us sat silently for some more time when the lights suddenly went off and we were plunged into a blanket of complete darkness. Involuntarily, a cry jutted out from my throat, "Who is it? Who is there?"

It seemed like somebody had intentionally shut off the main switch in the entire house, and we were left helpless inside the shroud of darkness. A burst of demonic laughter punctured through the dark sheath and echoed across the room. I had never seen any human who could laugh like that! It was horrendous. It was unending. It was ghastly.

Hehehehahahahahahaha . . .

It appeared as though a devilish apparition was laughing hysterically just outside the door! Satish quickly took out the battery-powered torch and flashed it at the door. Unfortunately, the outcome of that audacity was even more devastating. The laughter receded, but through an opposite window came a sharp, heartbreaking weep and moans of an unearthly voice that turned our blood cold. Such was the resonance of that penetrating lament in a feminine voice; it seemed that the entire bed was becoming wet in her tears! In an incomprehensible language, those despairs created heartbreaking anguish within our souls and stole away all our strengths and senses. It felt like an overdose of chloroform that was making us numb and lifeless.

Satish was braver than me. In a helpless struggle, he projected the torchlight upon the entire bed and screeched, "Who is there? Tell me, who is it?"

Nothing came into sight. No one answered his call. In that darkness, we both felt paralyzed. Suddenly, the bed started to jolt across the room and bang itself against the walls. Numerous skeletal phantoms began a surreal dance all around it. The cacophony of their crackling bones tore through our eardrums. The otherworldly opera made us feel as though our hearts would burst open in that tremor and bring our untimely deaths!

Then, the two of us became unconscious.

*

What happened thereafter was completely beyond my comprehension. As I opened my eyes, I realized that I was far away from home, in a distant land across the seven oceans. Possibly, I was magically transported to the inner chamber of a Chinese household. Within that little dark room, a dim lamp was flickering. I fathomed that it was well past midnight. As my eyes adjusted, I saw that within that dingy room, a frail emaciated old man was counting his final moments and was lying on the floor.

I looked at his sick and pale face and felt a pinning pain of remorse. Maybe, a prolonged illness had converted him into a haggard skeleton. Beside him, sat a plump woman, who was probably his wife. She was about four times the size of her husband, and she sat slouching upon an enormous wooden stool. Neither of them were visibly aware of our presence.

My eyes wandered across the room and I was astounded as I saw our very own mysterious bedstead beside them. I was shocked . . . *Who brought this bed into this room, afar across the seven oceans in this Chinese household?'*

My thought was interrupted abruptly when the enormous woman yawned monstrously and snapped her fingers so heavily that the sound reverberated across the room. As her sleepiness waned a little, she turned her eyes across the room.

In the meantime, the ailing man got up from the floor and staggered toward the bed with stealthy tiptoes. The woman was startled momentarily, but almost immediately returned to her conscious state and pounced upon him like a furious tigress! Spellbound, I sat and watched. The woman dragged her husband away from the bed and flung him upon the mattress on the floor, where he had been reclined earlier.

The woman growled fiercely while her husband pleaded earnestly with his fragile body and soul. In his desperate appeals, he feebly pointed toward the bed, as if it was his beloved possession, and he begged for one last chance to stretch upon the bed before he died. Sadly, the merciless woman objected even more viciously, and prevented him from even touching the bed with his sick fingers.

The intense scuffle brewed up like a storm, while the excitement became too much for the frail body of the old man. In a fit of lethal cough, he spewed blood! I shuddered at the sight. And then, the man's lifeless body fell, with his head sagged upon the bed, perhaps, for the last time. Devastated at the sight, his wife thumped down on the bed, and began to weep inconsolably.

Maybe, the heart-rending sight again took away my consciousness and I fainted.

*

When I regained consciousness, I saw that the first rays of dawn had already peeped in, and the sunlight of a new morning was flooded in every direction. I opened my eyes and saw that Satish's mother was sprinkling water over my face while she stooped over me anxiously.

She howled as she saw me open my eyes, "Khagen! My son, how are you? Khagen . . ."

"Where am I?" I asked feebly. I was still feeling very weak.

"You are downstairs, in our living room." she replied worriedly.

"Where is Satish?" I inquired agitatedly.

"He is still unconscious," she answered restlessly.

Thereafter, I listened to the horrendous tale of our previous night's ordeal. Around four o' clock in the morning, the two of us came down the stairs as though we were in a state of complete shock and hallucination. Then, we both fainted on the floor, near the front door. On hearing our faint wails, Satish's mother came out of her room. Our destitute condition made her frantic; she sat down near us and began to cry helplessly. Upon hearing her voice, the neighbors rushed in to help us. After almost three hours of supervision, I regained consciousness. The doctor had visited us and said, "They are out of danger now. It is a case of sudden shock. When they become conscious, give them some bromide."

On gaining consciousness, Satish, too, was bewildered like me. We were both indeed in a state of shock. I sat there dumbfounded, without uttering a single word.

Satish's mother yelled, "Throw away that cursed bed right away! I shall not tolerate it even for a single moment."

Soon, an advertisement was placed in the newspaper to sell off the phantom bed. The next evening, a huge crowd of prospective buyers arrived. Finally, the bed was sold for two thousand rupees. A Jew purchased and took it away.

Well, amid all the turmoil, Satish gained a little monetary profit by ultimately selling the bed, else he would have had no other option but to discard it without a single rupee in exchange.

Even after so many years, when the memories about that phantom bed fly past my mind, I can experience the shivers of the pinning trauma.

At times, I cannot help but wonder . . .

Where is that ghostly bedstead now? What happened to the haggard soul of that ailing Chinese man whose wife desperately stopped him to even touch his beloved bed?

Petrified by his disease, she shunned him from the final embrace of his beloved bed. Is that haunting spirit still roaming as an unsatisfied apparition?

Is he still chasing his beloved bed every night to prevent anybody else from enjoying its ethereal comfort?'

The answers are still a mystery, just like the mysterious phantom bed.

***

Gangadhar's Calamity

This is a story that dates back to the time when horse-drawn trams used to ferry across the streets of Calcutta. Gangadhar Kundu was an aging businessman in the Posta locality where he owned a small *masala dokaan*[2]. His ancestral village was somewhere in the Hooghly District, near Champadanga. He was a little over fifty years of age, but recent ailing health, coupled with a downturn in business, made him weaker; it made him feel sicker with every passing day.

One afternoon, Gangadhar sat and pondered, "I must do something to overcome these hurdles. The shop's rents are due for two months. The landlord's agent threatened that he would come in the evening to collect the money. What would I tell him then?"

Gangadhar was tense. His mind floated around options that could save him from his despondent condition. Suddenly, he remembered an old acquaintance. His name was Khudadad Khan,

---

[2] Spice shop.

the Muslim moneylender of Peshawari origin, who lived in the Metiabruz locality of the city. Gangadhar had dealt with the man earlier. He had borrowed money from him and repaid him too. But his interest rates were always too high, so in recent years, Gangadhar had refrained from borrowing from Khudadad.

Gangadhar contemplated the options and then headed out toward Metiabruz. He sighed, "Even though the interest rate is high, I don't have any other alternative. I must bring the money home by this evening."

It took him a while to locate Khudadad Khan's new residence. By the time the deal was done, and the money was received, it was late. Metiabruz was far from his home. The hour of dusk had arrived, and Gangadhar needed to cross the Kati Ganga (the name given to the portion of the Hooghly River near the Kidderpore locality of Calcutta) and then take the tramcar to return home.

Gangadhar was hurrying back when suddenly a stranger called him, "*Sahib*! Oh, Sahib, listen to me. Come here, please."

The evening had already descended and the place from where the stranger was talking to him was shadowed behind a crowd of trees and shrubbery. The place was secluded, with no other human being in sight. Gangadhar was carrying a good amount of money, too. A natural sense of suspicion and apprehension touched his heart. However, before he could react, the man came nearer. Strangely, it seemed as if the stranger was waiting behind those trees in his anticipation only.

The man was very tall and had unkempt, curly hair that reached down to his shoulders. In the obscure darkness, his face was not clearly visible. The man wore a traditional but shabby *ejar* and *alkhalla* dress and frowned at him. With a low, husky voice, he spoke with Gangadhar in a blend of Hindi and crude Bengali, "*Babu*, I shall give you a stash at a very good price! Would you like to buy the parcel? It is really cheap."

"What stash? What sort of parcel?" asked Gangadhar with astonishment.

The man took a cautious look around and then replied, "Not here. I cannot speak at this place. The police guards are all around. Come with me."

A curious Gangadhar followed him. As they reached the dark corner, near the trees and shrubbery, the stranger said, "It is cocaine! The stash has been smuggled out from the docks after dodging customs clearances! I shall give it to you secretly."

Gangadhar stood flabbergasted. He had never done such underhanded business. He again contemplated, "Smuggled cocaine! Oh God, this is dangerous! No, I shall not buy it."

The stranger, who seemed to be a Punjabi Muslim, stared at him and asked earnestly in his unpolished Bengali accent, "Babu, you take it. Trust me. It will be good for you. I would charge you a minimal price for such a fantastic item. I am in a difficult position, and I am unable to find a good customer. Sahib, I have been roaming around in search of somebody to sell this cocaine, but the perils are high, and I cannot visit everywhere. The policemen are on the lookout, and I need to be cautious. They are on high alert to seek us out. None of my acquaintances are even talking to me. I don't know why the entire city is suddenly so intimidated by the fear of the police! I have visited people with whom I had prior business dealings, but they are not even looking at me! Babu, please don't refuse this offer. First, see the stash and then we can bargain a good price for you."

There was a magnetic charm in the stranger's voice that touched Gangadhar's heart. He stood blankly for a few moments and deliberated . . . *Many have become overnight millionaires in the shady business of cocaine. Without courage, success and profits remain distant. Has anyone ever become rich without taking a risk? Let's see what destiny has in store for me . . .*

As he looked up, Gangadhar was startled to see that the man had suddenly vanished! A moment ago, he was standing right in front of Gangadhar. How could he suddenly evaporate within the darkness? With a fear of being noticed by suspicious eyes, Gangadhar couldn't call out aloud. He just whispered, "Where are you? Khan Sahib, where did you go?"

As his eyes scanned the entire surrounding and his gaze returned, he was even more surprised to see the stranger standing right in front of him. Within the darkness, the tall Khan Sahib seemed to have disappeared and then reappeared like some ethereal being.

Without wasting time, Gangadhar said in his crude Hindi, "Alright then, let's go fast. I have a long to go back home."

Nonetheless, an uncanny feeling lingered in Gangadhar's mind. The stranger was desperately trying to hide something. He replied with a smirk, "Yes, follow me. I will show you the cocaine."

The two of them started to pace down the banks of Kati Ganga. In the prevalent obscurity of the evening, they went far. At the time, that locality was mostly uninhabited. A few big and small boats were scattered along the muddy banks. A few empty workshops—perhaps abandoned by the blacksmiths—remained dispersed along the way. Unkempt shrubbery of thorns and wild bushes girdled the surrounding. Far away, the distant lights of Kidderpore Bazaar were visible like twinkling stars.

Suddenly, Khan Sahib asked a peculiar question, "Babu, are you able to see me?"

"Why won't I?" asked Gangadhar irritably, "I am not so old that my eyesight would fail me during the evening."

They continued to walk silently. Then, a bit later, Gangadhar asked, "Khan Sahib, where do you live?"

With lightning speed, the man turned back, looked at him suspiciously and asked, "Why? What will you do? Are you planning to inform the police about my hideout? If you have any such malicious plans, then I am warning you in advance! The consequences wouldn't be very healthy for you. I will hand you over the cocaine and you will pay me in return. Take your stash and go back. Why do you need to know where I live?"

The glint in his eyes was razor sharp and Gangadhar didn't get a good vibe about it. Again, he felt a blatant discomfort in the company of the strange man. Eerily, the man was not even properly visible in those obscure barren surroundings.

Gangadhar felt insecure, and the pangs of fear grazed past his skin. Particularly because he had a significant amount of money with him—that he had just borrowed from Khudadad Khan—and in such a situation, he had come so far with a stranger. Gangadhar cursed himself for his overpowering greed that had made him take such a decision.

As they walked without uttering a word to each other, Gangadhar sensed a sharp touch of uncanniness in his companion. Gangadhar felt uneasy about the intentions of the man, but he dared not to do anything. He was afraid that the man might be deceiving him to a secluded place to usurp the cash he was carrying. He feared that the man, being much stronger than him, could easily overpower and murder him!

'Yes, greed often makes a man lose his sanity!' he cursed himself, *'I should have been in my senses. Now that I have already embarked upon this spooky journey, the dangers are bound to augment. What if he takes out a dagger? No, I must remain cautious!'*

In a state of trance, Gangadhar continued to follow the man toward his secret hideout. After crossing a vast meadow, they arrived at a dilapidated and abandoned warehouse. A broken tree trunk was lying astray at a little distance from its entrance. As they reached, Khan Sahib asked Gangadhar to sit down and then quickly vanished somewhere in the darkness. A distraught

Gangadhar looked around scarily. The forsaken warehouse was surrounded by an overgrowth of trees, grass, and weeds. The place was completely abandoned.

However, darkness seemed a bit thinner in that open meadow. In that thin obscurity, Gangadhar looked at the old warehouse carefully and comprehended that it had been deserted for many years. The bamboo fence was completely ruined while the roof of the ramshackle warehouse had fallen off in multiple places. Even the front door was in a despicable state and was damaged beyond repair.

An elusive fear was gradually gripping Gangadhar from within. His mind questioned his own rationality. Why did he come to such a shadowy place all alone, that too, when he was carrying a huge amount of cash with him?

He reasoned back. He wouldn't have ever done such a mindless thing! He was not new to the city. He was a seasoned businessman. Then, why did he do it? Yes, there was a distinctive magical magnetism in the words of that stranger, Khan Sahib, that had pulled Gangadhar with an invisible strength. The poor man didn't have the power to resist it. That was the only explanation! Otherwise, why would he come along with a stranger and risk his own life?

Precipitously, with an abrupt speed, the figure of Khan Sahib condensed from within the thin darkness and stood right in front of Gangadhar.

'The silent movement of the man is so suspicious! He seems to evaporate into the air and then reappear with equal swiftness! It never seemed that he went anywhere. It seemed as though he was omnipresent around me and had just vanished and resurfaced . . .' wondered Gangadhar with an alarm.

An unperturbed Khan Sahib opened the crumbling front door and entered slowly. Gangadhar sensed a subtle numbness across his entire body while his heart palpitated with fear within his ribcage. He felt that his evil companion would grasp his throat with his huge hands to choke him or dab a dagger through his heart to murder him brutally.

He shuddered with the thought. *That was the sinister plan of the villain! I am sure he knew that I had a big amount of cash with me. Who knows, he might be an accomplice of Khudadad Khan himself! Oh God, what a calamity has befallen me!'*

Drops of sweat crowded across his forehead. For once, he considered running away as fast as he could. But the other moment, he knew that he was an old man and was no match for the powerful enemy who could easily defeat him in such a fruitless race. It was an impossible idea.

Like a puppet, Gangadhar followed his companion and entered the warehouse. As he went in, another sight stunned him. The opposite wall of the warehouse was completely broken. Gradually, Gangadhar was able to see in the darkness. Amid that hazy visibility, he could look at the surroundings within the warehouse. The entire place was in ruins, and there were two large empty jars scattered carelessly around a corner. Invisible cobwebs freckled almost every empty spot of the place. A damp stench overwhelmed the air within, and the uneven floor, too, seemed somewhat wet. It was evident that the place had been devoid of human presence for a very long time.

Now, where did Khan Sahib go? Where did he vanish again?' wondered Gangadhar, as he felt irritated as well as afraid.

A few minutes passed, but nobody could be seen anywhere around. Gangadhar stood there, all alone, in that eerily stranded warehouse. Once again, an unknown fear gripped him. It was a unique fear, just like the cold touch of a paranormal entity. It was a bizarre wave of panic, as if an unsettling omen presaged a ghastly catastrophe.

Gangadhar felt an icy cold tempest brewing within his ribcage. He got more and more perplexed. He failed to understand the nature of the fear that he was experiencing, but he knew he was very scared. A sudden gust of freezing wind began to blow within the warehouse.

After some more time, Gangadhar could again see Khan Sahib again. He was standing right in front of him. Once more, the creepy man coagulated out from the thin air!

Unexpectedly and even more suspiciously, Khan Sahib screeched, "Are you deaf? I have been talking to you for such a long time, and you haven't heard even a single word of mine! Did you not hear me? If yes, then why are you not answering?"

Gangadhar looked puzzled, while Khan Sahib continued, "Were you able to locate the place where the cocaine is hidden? Take that shovel and lift those jars! Don't just stand like a joker and waste my time!"

Gangadhar was astonished. When did Khan Sahib say all that? Was he a madman? When did he say so many things, and Gangadhar didn't even notice?

Puzzled by the strange situation, Gangadhar replied, "When did you show me the place where the cocaine is hidden? And where is the shovel?"

As Gangadhar looked up toward Khan Sahib, he witnessed the ghastliest specter in front of his eyes! In an otherworldly instance, the entire face, neck, bosom, limbs . . . The entire body of Khan Sahib began to fall apart like a crumbling sand castle in front of a storm! The horrifying spectacle unfolded while a gale seemed to blow away each disintegrated particle of that paranormal dust. Khan Sahib desperately struggled to prevent his own ghostly body from falling into pieces, but, he failed to do so. One by one, the paranormal wind blew away every particle while Khan Sahib—the otherworldly apparition—shrieked mutely in his futile battle.

Then, as that ghastly storm was over, Khan Sahib was gone. He had crumbled down into dust. A shaken Gangadhar stood alone within that eerily dark paranormal warehouse. Suddenly, another burst of icy wind blew past Gangadhar and touched his face like a slap with the cold bony fingers of a skeleton. That last jolt was enormous for his nerves, and Gangadhar fainted on the damp floor of the warehouse.

A local boat of fishermen was docked somewhere along the Kati Ganga. By a stroke of luck, the fishermen recovered Gangadhar from that eerie warehouse while he was unconscious. Why and how? Gangadhar could never find out. Those benevolent fishermen discovered his address and took him home on that night of calamity. Though Gangadhar didn't lose a single rupee that night, his body and soul were shattered by the shock. It took him almost a month to recover.

Two Months Later . . .

Gangadhar went to Metiabruz to repay his debt and told Khudadad Khan about whatever had happened on that fateful night. The latter listened to him quietly and then sat somberly for some time.

After a while, Khudadad said, "Sahib, that man was Ameer Khan! He was a big dealer of smuggled cocaine. He had a big business. Years ago, a ship was docked in the harbor and from there, he could smuggle a good quantity of the stash. Nobody knew where he used to hide those smuggled items. No one could ever find out."

Khudadad looked at Gangadhar and continued, "In the middle of that same month, Ameer Khan was murdered. Neither the police nor anyone else could discover who had committed the crime. However, it was evident that one of his evil accomplices had done that gory job.

Khudadad shuddered while he spoke, "Sahib, I believe that the ghost of Ameer Khan is still roaming around in the darkness and is trying to sell off his stash of cocaine! That elusive and tarnished cocaine is not letting his spirit escape! Sahib, do you remember where he took you? Do you remember the location of that warehouse? Can you take me there?"

Unfortunately , Gangadhar was totally oblivious to where he had been on that fateful night. He shook his head to say 'No'. Well, even if he ever remembered, Gangadhar would have never dared to tread those ghostly quarters again!

As he walked back from Metiabruz, Gangadhar remembered the face of Khan Sahib, his paranormal companion of that scary night. It seemed to him as though the face of the man was slowly getting reflected in the darkness. He remembered the inhuman struggle of Khan Sahib—within his momentarily visible human face—and how he failed to fulfill his final desire.

Was he still roaming as an undead or a vagrant spirit? Was the ghost of the drug peddler, Khan Sahib, still in search of his secret stash of cocaine?

***

Fate of the
Intoxicated Hunter

The Mouchaak Magazine approached me for a story, and the Editor had written that he preferred a tale of the paranormal. I, Animesh Banerjee, had sent it to them, but it was not a ghost story . . . It was an account of a real incident that revealed a blatant truth . . .

Years ago, when I was employed at the Lahore Museum, I was good friends with Mr Vinayak Dutta Singh, who was the editor of the renowned *Deshbandhu* newspaper of Lahore. Mr Singh belonged to a noble origin and was a descendant of an eminent family. His ancestors were not from Punjab. They belonged to Kota Durbar in Rajputana. Three generations ago, to fulfill the duties of state affairs, his grandfather relocated to Punjab, and his family continued to live away from their homeland thereafter.

Every evening, it was my customary habit to visit Mr Singh at his residence. Sitting inside his parlor, I used to be mesmerized by the enthralling collection of antiques that adorned the decorated walls of that sprawling room. The vintage opulence of ancient armors, weapons, axes, maces, flags, and many such antiques continued to fascinate me as I used to gulp down the overdose of valiant tales about the Rajputs and their valorous antiquity. The stories brought life into those ancient objects as I sat and listened to the tales from Mr Singh, who was immensely proficient in his storytelling with his deep knowledge about the history of Kota Durbar.

Well, as brevity is the soul of wit, I must now reveal a bizarre account that is etched clearly into my mind. If the renowned and respectable Mr Vinayak Dutta Singh hadn't told it to me directly, I would have never believed it. Narrated by Mr Singh himself, this story is deemed to be true, despite all the bizarreness within it. And that is why I chose to send this story to the *Mouchaak* magazine.

On a freezing winter evening, when the temperature had dropped and the chill in the air was biting, I went to Mr Singh's parlor for my routine evening meet up. After a cup of hot tea and few puffs of excellent tobacco, I looked at Mr Singh and asked with a sudden fancy, "Sir, do you believe in evil spirits or demonic creatures?"

Mr Singh was a non-smoker. He looked back at me somberly and replied in his heavy voice, "Yes, I do."

I asked enthusiastically, "Have you ever seen a ghost or any paranormal entity?"

Mr Singh remained somber and responded, "No, I am not talking about my own experience. I am talking about an incident that took place in my grandfather's younger brother's life. In fact, if that fateful incident hadn't taken place, our family would've been among the most aristocratic *Talukdar*[3] families of Kota Durbar.

---

[3] A term that was used to designate families of the aristocratic ruling class during the Bengal Sultanate.

"Then, come along with me, I will give you a good tip. What do you say?" grinned Singh Sahib sarcastically.

"Pardon me please, even if you give me a hundred rupees, I won't go to the Nahara Lake at night. Hazoor, we are men of the Bheel tribes; we don't fear tigers. With these hands, I have killed many of those beasts with mere arrows. But Sahib, in this strange world, aren't there creatures that are dreaded more than tigers?"

Singh Sahib was not very familiar with the terrains around the Nahara Nipaat because the lake was located about forty miles away from his own province. He left the village of the Bheel tribes and traveled about eight miles afoot to cross the hills and reach the flatlands. At a distance, the rippling salt water of the enormous lake was sparkling in the bright sunlight. The woods along the banks of that huge lake were completely forsaken of any human presence.

Upon reaching the lake, Singh-Sahib found there was plenty of daylight left and he quickly made a makeshift canopy with wild bulrush and foliage. Then, along with his rifle, he hid himself inside that shade so that the flocks of geese wouldn't notice his unwanted presence.

Soon, the dark cover of the evening spread across the entire landscape. The soft moonlight came alive and perforated the dark sheath of the night. A flock of wild parrots flew over the sparkling water of the lake and then vanished into the woods. The area surrounding woods became noiseless in that sleepy haze. The moonlight sparkled upon the water, giving it a silvery hue. As the night deepened, the chill in the air became bitter. Two days ago, it was the last full moon night of autumn.

The wintry chills were a summon that it was time for the wild geese to arrive at the lake. However, no one came along.

Singh Sahib wondered, "What is happening? Why aren't the geese coming?"

In his restless mind, the words of old Bhaijee reverberated . . . *'Hazoor, remember, on nights when the wild geese descend on the lake's water, you can be assured that no horrors will intrude upon that place . . .'*

"What horrors loom over if the wild geese don't turn up?" Singh Sahib questioned in his own mind, "Tigers would come from the hilly woods to drink water from the lake?"

Gradually, the night grew deeper while the soft moonlight scintillated upon the rippling water of the lake. Strewed in the shimmery moonlight, the vast stretches of the barren desert appeared mysteriously stunning while a teething silence grasped the entire area. Singh Sahib was a valiant and fearless man, but in that strange and wild nocturnal backdrop, even he felt a bit creepy. The eerie white cloak of the moon's silver glow had a strange supernatural aura.

Singh Sahib took out his leather-covered bottle of whisky and drank down a few gulps. The golden fluid passed down his throat and warmed his body.

Suddenly, he looked at the western corner of the lake and his heart was filled with excitement. Across the lake, he could see a flock of wild geese slowly descending toward the water. Their stunning white wings dazzled with moonshine. Gradually, they came down and sat scattered over the sandy banks of Nahara Lake.

The place where the geese sat was about a little more than two hundred square yards from Singh Sahib's canopy. It was nearly impossible to get a good range with the rifle from that distance during the night.

Singh Sahib pondered, "Let me wait and see if more flocks will come down at a closer distance. Patience is a virtue for a hunter. It is wise to quietly observe the geese."

However, the next moment, he felt dumbfounded. He was unable to believe what he was seeing! In his astonishment, he rubbed his eyes several times . . .

He thought, *'What is happening? What sort of geese are these? I may have gulped down a little whisky, but that shouldn't blur my vision! How can my vision become incoherent with such a small amount of alcohol?'*

With surprise, Singh Sahib observed that those birds were not common wild geese. They were unusually large. Even their behavior was different and mysterious. The next moment, he perceived with a greater shock that the surreal creatures weren't just birds. They were bizarre aviator creatures with humanlike faces and features!

Singh Sahib rubbed his eyes once more and speculated, "What is happening to me tonight?"

Moments later, the creatures came down into the water, swam like wild geese, and reached close to the bank where Singh Sahib was hiding inside the canopy.

In that soft white moonlight, the reckless, fearless, and inebriated Singh Sahib saw with terror and disbelief that those creatures weren't wild geese, but a group of beautiful women! In their resplendent white attires—that were shimmering in the moonlight—their feminine laughter and their exceptionally attractive countenances appeared surrealistically heavenly!

They played carelessly with each other in a strange ecstasy and swam silently with their sensuous bodies across the lake, like a wedge of beautiful swans. Singh Sahib couldn't perceive how long that otherworldly game of the supernatural nymphs continued.

Following that, those creatures stretched their large white wings, flew across the moonlit sky and vanished. The air around the Nahara Lake remained soaked in the sweet intoxicating fragrance of their divine bodies.

A bewildered Singh Sahib pinched himself to check if he was dreaming. He was unable to believe what he had seen with his own eyes. By that time, the effect of alcohol had evaporated from his body, and he was totally in his senses. Yet, he was still in a state of amazement about what he had witnessed. Soon, the first light of dawn perforated the darkness, and a baffled Singh Sahib walked in a puzzled state up to the foothills of the mountains. From there, somehow, he managed to reach the village of the Bheel tribes.

Old Bhaijee asked apprehensively, "Hazoor, did the wild geese descend on the lake's water?"

That day, Singh Sahib lied to him. He said that the wild geese did descend on the lake's water, but he had been unable to hunt any of them. Spellbound by an unknown power, he chose not to reveal anything else. He remained silent about the bizarre incident that he had witnessed during the night. From that day onwards, a strange enticement began to pull him. His subconscious voice told him . . . *'I must visit Nahara Nipaat again! I know, if I reveal the truth, then Bhaijee would never let me do it!'*

Nonetheless, that night, the flock of wild geese descended on the lake's water, again. They were a flock of real wild geese. Then, for the next few nights, the same thing happened. Groups of wild geese came down to the lake while Singh Sahib sat restlessly, waiting inside his canopy of wild bulrush. He felt reluctant to shoot them with his rifle while his heart yearned for one more glimpse of the ethereal fairies he had seen on that fateful night.

Then, one night, once again those otherworldly nymphs came down over the lake. Bathed in the soft sparkling moonlight, once again, they were heavenly attractive to look at. That night, they came closer to Singh Sahib's canopy. They swam along the bank, beside the overgrown wild grass, like beautiful and elegant swans. Their stunningly beautiful faces overwhelmed Singh Sahib's heart.

Suddenly, a few hours before dawn, a wild fancy engrossed Singh Sahib's senses. Was it the effect of alcohol or some untamed impulse? I don't know . . . Singh Sahib leapt out from the canopy and ran madly toward the water . . . toward those nymphs! Maybe, in a reckless frenzy, he wanted to touch and hold one of them.

The abrupt intrusion created a nervous turmoil. Like frightened wild geese, they swam away and dispersed far and wide across the waters of Nahara Nipaat. Then, they fluttered their wings wide, hovered out from the water, and flew away. In that restive moonlit night, they vanished into thin air.

The next afternoon, Singh Sahib was found in a state of absolute lunacy, somewhere near the banks of the Nahara Nipaat. A fisherman found him roaming around aimlessly across the desolate lands and brought him to the village of the Bheel tribes.

Old Bhaijee lamented, "Hazoor didn't pay heed to my caution. I had told him, the nights when flocks of geese don't descend upon the lake, those nights are full of horror!"

Sometimes, Singh Sahib used to get sane, but that never lasted for long. Soon, he would submerge in a state lunacy. In those brief moments of sanity, he had narrated that bizarre incident many times to his family. Ten years before his death, he became a complete madman, and he never recovered from that insanity.

*

Vinayak Dutta Singh finished his story and sat in silence.

I was speechless when I heard the story. I said softly, "It is indeed a strange incident. But . . ."

Vinayak Dutta Singh replied, "But . . . in this twentieth century, it is a story that is hard to believe, right? Yes, I know that too. Yet, please note Mr Banerjee, this is a fifty-year-old story that I just narrated. Some say that the sight of those ethereal nymphs was a result of Singh Sahib's excessive alcoholism. In his intoxicated state, he must have mistaken the wild geese to be otherworldly nymphs. While some say the sight of ethereal nymphs dooms human beings into lunacy!"

Old Bheel Bhaijee used to whisper the same words of caution . . . "Hazoor, remember, on nights when the wild geese descend on the lake's water, you can be assured that no horrors will intrude upon that place . . ."

The invisible distinction between natural and supernatural was and remains an inexplicable mystery that is beyond the comprehension of the human mind.

***

A Fabled Curse

Once, a bizarre incident took place in my life . . .

It happened about three or four years ago. Due to some work, I had to visit the Barisal region. From a *ganj*[4] in that province, at about noon, I got onto a boat. With me, there was another traveler who belonged to Barisal. As the vessel sailed, a jolly conversation unfolded between us, and time began to pass easily. That year, the Durga Puja festival had just come to an end and the sky was mostly cloudy throughout the day. Intermittent showers of rain continued to drizzle all day, but during the evening, the sky was clear. Soon, through the broken bits of clouds across the sky, a sweet silvery hue of the moonlight peeped out.

Once the evening descended, our vessel left the main river and entered a narrow creek. We learned that

---

[4] It is a common suffix/prefix meaning 'treasured place' or 'neighborhood' in Hindi, Bengali, and Urdu, used in the names of *bazaars*, *mandi*, marketplaces and towns in India and Bangladesh. Here, it denotes a town.

the creek goes past the Noakhali region and ends at the Meghna River. It was my first visit to Eastern Bengal, and everything was very new to me. As we sailed, I gulped down the overdose of vastness within those picturesque landscape. It felt fresh and soothed my eyes. Eventually, darkness enveloped the landscapes. Along that narrow creek, in the dark night, the screwpine woods on both the sides gleamed under the gentle moonlight that peeped through the clouds. A few large and open fields were visible along the banks. At places, random woods of wild turmeric, cane, and fern came along to greet us. It seemed as though they were bending over to touch the water's surface.

There was a chill in the air and it felt a bit cold, but I chose to sit outside the awning of our boat and enjoy the rustic nocturnal beauty of the countryside.

The region of Barisal, near the Sundarbans, was speckled with numerous creeks and rivulets and was not far from the ocean's bay. The islands of Hatia and Sandwip weren't very far either. As the night deepened a bit more, the adjacent woods—along the banks of the narrow creek—appeared surreal in the moonshine. The region was almost uninhabited. Dense woodlands and marshes girdled the entire riverbank.

My companion, the other traveler, said, "It is late in the night. Please don't stay outside. Come, let's go inside. These are strange wild forests . . . don't you understand?"

Then, he started telling various stories related to the Sundarbans. One of his uncles was an officer of the forest department. Years ago, he had crossed the swampy waters of Sundarbans on one of the steamers of his uncle's office. With vigor, my companion continued to tell me the stories of his experiences.

Gradually, it was almost midnight.

There was only one old and frail oarsman who was sailing our boat. He came up and said in an equally frail voice, "Babu, we will soon arrive at the confluence of the big river. At this hour of the night, I don't think I would be able to tackle the boat in those deep currents. I shall halt the boat here for the night?"

Saying so, even though there was a question in his voice to seek our unsaid approval, he halted the boat at the bank of the creek and tied it. Soon, the moon too was cloaked behind the large trees. On both sides of the creek, the vast woods seemed shrouded in the dark cover of the night. A pinning silence engrossed everything around us. Even the buzzing world of insects was uncannily silent.

I asked my companion, "This is such a narrow creek; isn't it possible for a tiger to leap inside our boat?"

"I would be surprised if one of them doesn't," my companion replied in a nonchalant voice.

Hearing his blank and blatant reply, I felt ecstatic with terror, and crouched up inside the awning of our boat.

After a while, he said, "Come, let's lie down and rest a bit now. Even though it isn't possible to sleep at this hour and it isn't right to do so as well, we can at least close our eyes and rest for some time."

I followed his words, stretched my limbs, and sat down a bit more comfortably. After a while, I turned to call my companion and noticed that he was already fast asleep. The old oarsman was in deep sleep, too. I thought, *Why should I stay awake for nothing? The stalwarts traveling with me are sleeping without any worries, and I must follow suit too!*

What happened next, is a wild and uncanny experience of my entire life that I shall remember as long as I live . . .

Just as I was getting ready to sleep, a sudden eerie sound cut through the silent night and jolted my senses. It seemed to me as if somebody was playing a gramophone inside that enormous dark forest in the middle of the night.

Hurriedly, driven by a sudden sense of urgency, I jumped and sat up. I wondered . . . *'Is that the sound of a gramophone? How is that possible? In this dense and uninhabited forest, at who would play a gramophone at this hour?'*

I calmed my mind and listened carefully. No, it wasn't the sound of a gramophone. Amidst the dense growth of the Indian Oak and the littoral forest, someone was shrieking in a high-pitched and heart-wrenching voice! Apparently, the sound was a chorus of multiple voices. When one listens to the sound of a gramophone being played at a distance, it is usually a subtle muffled tone. As I heard the shrieks, it was a similar mixture of audible and inaudible pitches. For a moment, I thought I heard a few familiar Bengali words too, but I was unable to recognize them. The uncanny sound persisted for about a minute, and then, once again, everything became soundless.

In a state of shock and surprise, I came out in the open from the awning of our boat. The dark night was like an impenetrable blanket that concealed everything around us. The surrounding woods were absolutely quiet. Only the sound of the water under the boat was mutely audible. At a distance, the trunks of the large Indian Oak trees stood like veiled apparitions.

I thought . . . *'Let me wake up my companion . . .'*

Nonetheless, the next moment my mind told me, *'Why wake up the poor guy? He is sleeping soundly. Instead, let me stay awake and remain alert.'*

I stood outside the awning and lit a cigarette. As I finished smoking and was about to re-enter the boat, a shrill, uncanny, and heart-wrenching shriek reverberated like a massive buzz of millions of crickets buzzing together! The unnerving shriek pierced through the dark night's sheath across the vast wilderness around us. It seemed as though some ghostly arrows of dissonance were supernaturally dispersed across the sky . . .

Ohh, you who have come, Ohh, passing traveler . . . Take us out from this hell. Ohh, passing boatmen and sailors . . . come and save us! Please save us . . .

The old oarsman suddenly woke up with a freaking scare. I pushed my companion, who was still fast asleep, and said, "Hey! Wake up . . . wake up!"

The frightened oarsman shuddered and said in a shaky voice, "Oh Lord! *Babu*, did you hear that?"

My companion woke up in shock and asked, "What happened? Why did you wake me up? Is everything alright? Has any wild animal jumped aboard?"

Quickly, I divulged everything that had happened. He listened to me and hurriedly went out in the open.

Then, the three of us stood quietly outside the awning of the boat and tried to listen to the sounds. The lack of any noise made the atmosphere even more uncomfortable. Despite the restless ripples of the high tide, which were lashing against the bottom of our boat, the entire surrounding was, once again, eerily silent.

My companion asked the oarsman, "Is this, then . . .?"

"Yes, Babu," replied the visibly scared oarsman, "on our left is the *Gor of Kirti Pasha*! Babu, it is that that fabled moat . . ."

My companion became infuriated and said, "You're such a stupid man! Why did you dock the boat in this place, that too in the middle of the night? I can't believe that you're so mindless!"

The old oarsman got tearful and replied, "Babu, please forgive me. I took this decision because the three of us are together. Moreover, I don't have the strength to tackle the powerful high tides in the big river."

I was listening to their weird conversation, and I asked my companion, "What is the matter? Do you know anything about all this?"

More than fear, I was unnerved by the suddenness of the situation.

My companion commanded the oarsman, "The night is long. Take out your kerosene lamp. We shall ignite the lamp and sit near it."

I asked the oarsman, "Did you, too, hear the strange sounds?"

"Yes, Babu," he replied in a shaky voice, "My sleep was interrupted when I heard that. I am well acquainted with it. I have heard those weird sounds while sailing along this creek before as well."

My companion sighed and added, "This is a peculiar phenomenon of these quarters. However, since this place is located near the borders of the Sundarbans and is largely uninhabited, the legend is mostly prevalent among sailors who sail their boat across this region. Although, there is a history behind this legend, but the sailors are not familiar with that history. Let me tell you about it . . ."

We sat around the vaporous glow of the kerosene lamp, inside the heart of the Sundarbans forests, and listened to the bizarre legend of the Gor of Kirti Pasha!

*

Three hundred years ago, Munim Khan was the *Subedar*[5] of Gour. Vast provinces of Bengal were then under the control of the *Baro-Bhuiyans*[6]. The said provinces near the Sundarbans were under the command of two such Bhuiyans, named Raja Ramchandra Ray and Isha Khan. Outside the confluence of the Meghna River, in the ocean's bay—the place that is now popularly known as Sandwip Channel—was the favorite haunt of fierce Arakanese and

---

[5] Subedar is a historical civil or military rank initially relating to a senior official of the Mughal Empire who governed an assigned 'subha' (province).

[6] The Baro-Bhuiyans were confederacies of soldier-landowners in Assam and Bengal in the late Middle Ages and the early modern period. The confederacies consisted of loosely independent entities, each led by a warrior chief or a landlord.

Portuguese pirates. Those ruthless villains used to lurk relentlessly in those waters in search of coveted prey.

Back in those days, the place was not completely covered in dense forests. The entire place belonged to the territory of *zamindar*[7] Kirti Ray. His huge fortress existed proudly across the regions around the creek. Kirti Ray had fought many battles with the Arakanese and Portuguese pirates. His personal army and naval fleet commanded a battalion of valiant soldiers, and boasted of guns, canons, and warships. Sandwip was then the main abode of Portuguese pirates. Every zamindar of the nearby provinces needed to maintain a strong personal army to protect themselves from those wicked pirates. On the western side of the woods, at that time, existed another creek, which too led to the main river.

Kirti Ray was a brutal and unconquerable zamindar whose villainous majesty was infamous. It was fabled that, in his kingdom, there didn't exist any young and beautiful damsel who didn't pay a visit to his personal chambers. In a way, he too was no less than an evil pirate. Kirti Ray owned a fleet of small fast fast-going longboats and gunboats, which belonged to his personal navy. He used to employ that fleet to attack wealthy, but less powerful families in neighboring zamindari provinces and loot their wealth and women.

The zamindari adjacent to Kirti Ray's provinces belonged to one of his friends. They were the descendant of the leaseholders under Chandradwip's sovereign, Raja Ramchandra Ray. Upon the death of Kirti Ray's friend, the latter's son, Nar-Narayan Ray became the next zamindar. Nar-Narayan was a young man who was valiant, strong, fearless, and an able successor to his father. Furthermore, Nar-Narayan was also a dear friend of Kirti Ray's son Chanchal Ray.

---

[7] A zamindar in the Indian subcontinent was an autonomous or semi-autonomous ruler of a province.

Once, to honor the invitation of Kirti Ray, Nar-Narayan visited his zamindari for a couple of days. Chanchal Ray's young bride, Lakshmi Devi, became fond of her husband's dear friend. She began to admire him like her own brother-in-law. However, the overdose of that brotherly affection soon became a trouble for Nar-Narayan. He was a young man, but he possessed a serious personality. But Lakshmi Devi's sisterly pranks often led him to embarrassment. At times, his headdress would be lost and he would discover it under his own pillow after searching for it for hours. Or his favorite sword would vanish from his possession not once but as many as five times in a day! Even his paan would be magically filled with ingredients that are seldom found inside it. Bearing all these pranks silently, Nar-Narayan smilingly realized that his newly found sister-in-law was a mischievous young soul.

Chanchal Ray used to secretly laugh heartily at those pranks, but he told his wife, "Dear, please spare my innocent friend. He is our guest for a few days. The poor guy is clearly terrified by your mischiefs."

A few days later, upon an unexpected order from Kirti Ray, Chanchal Ray had to go away on an emergency expedition. After staying for a couple of more days, Nar-Narayan decided to return to his zamindari.

Before Nar-Narayan left, Lakshmi Devi told him with her mischievous smile, "Brother, next time, don't forget to bring along a wife who will keep an eye on your belongings. Alright? Hahaha . . ."

As his entourage set sail, and Nar-Narayan Ray's budgerow had just crossed the confluence of the Ray-Mangal River, they were attacked by pirates. The hour was a little past noon and the blazing sunlight reflected on the water, making it look like the shining blade of a sword. Across the ocean, there was no other ship that could come to help Nar-Narayan and his men. The place was just off the coast of the main abode of the pirates, and the villains swarmed around the budgerow fiercely. A bloody battle ensued and almost all Nar-Narayan Ray's men were either slaughtered or mortally wounded. Nar-Narayan himself fought valiantly, but a sudden lethal injury on his leg incapacitated him, and with an unbearable pain, he passed out.

When he regained consciousness, Nar-Narayan saw that he was lying inside a completely dark place. Above his eyes, there seemed to appear a light that looked like a large and bright star. After a while, he wiped his eyes and understood that it was not a star, it was a ray of light entering that dark place through a small opening above. Nar-Narayan comprehended that he was lying on the damp floor of a dark chamber with enormous walls filled with patches of moss. He was a prisoner inside that mysterious, dark, and deathly cavity.

A few more days passed. Nobody brought him any food or water. Nar-Narayan understood that whoever had imprisoned him inside that dark cell was determined to starve him to death. In front of him was his inevitable fate—a pitiless death.

Another day went by. In that unbearable pain from his festering wound, coupled with intolerable hunger and thirst, even the faint beam of light began to die away in front of his eyes. Lying helplessly on the cold stony floor of that massive chamber, a powerless Nar-Narayan awaited his imminent death. A subtle numbness overwhelmed his body and took him toward a deathly sleep. Perhaps, it was Mother Nature's dose of chloroform to provide an anesthetic sensation to a dying creature.

Suddenly, Nar-Narayan noticed a faint ray of light, and his comatose sleep was abruptly broken. In sheer surprise, he opened his eyes with all his strength and saw Lakshmi Devi standing in front of him. In her hands, she held a flickering earthen lamp. Nar-Narayan was about to say something, but Lakshmi Devi cautioned him to remain silent. Then, she covered the lamp with her sari and gestured for him to follow her.

Nar-Narayan doubted, *'Is this real, or a dream?'*

But, in the faint light of that flickering lamp, the damp, moss-ridden dark walls of that deathly cell told him, *'No . . . this is a harsh reality!'*

Nar-Narayan was a tough and brave man. Despite being overwhelmed by pain, hunger, and thirst, he got up quickly and with firm footsteps, retraced the path that Lakshmi Devi was quickly moving along. They went up a spiral staircase and passed through a long tunnel, and finally reached the banks of the creek outside the main palace of the fortress.

Lakshmi Devi took out a bag, gave it to Nar-Narayan and said, "There is food inside the bag. Don't have it now. You know how to swim, so don't waste any time. Jump into the water and swim to the other side as fast as possible. Once you reach there, eat some food from this bag and then run away as far as you can!"

Nar-Narayan was an intelligent man. He could comprehend what had happened. His province was adjacent to the zamindari of Kirti Ray. If he were dead, Kirti Ray would inevitably become the undisputed lord of both provinces. The huge domains and lands of his zamindari, his valiant army, his fleet of ships, and all the wealth of his family would incontestably pass onto Kirti Ray's possession. How could the merciless Kirti Ray leave any stone unturned to fulfill that greed? Such a possession would make Kirti Ray the strongest zamindar of the entire province.

In the faint light of the lamp, Nar-Narayan saw that the usual mischievous and jovial expression on Lakshmi Devi's face had evaporated. Instead, a dark shadow of fear had descended upon it. It was soaked in emotional sympathy with a motherly love and apprehension for him. The two of them stood covered in the dark blanket of the night while the current of the high tide pulled out the creek's water, which splashed noisily on the narrow banks.

Nar-Narayan asked anxiously with a heavy heart, "*Bouthakrun*[8], is Chanchal also involved in this conspiracy?"

"No, my brother," replied Lakshmi Devi, "he is innocent and is completely unaware of it. This is a dark conspiracy of my evil father-in-law. To fulfill his wicked motive, he sent your friend away! Now I know, it was a part of his devilish plan."

Nar-Narayan saw that her face was red with embarrassment. She confessed, "I came to know about this murderous plan today itself. The leader of the sentinels, who guard the backdoors of the palace, reveres me like a mother. With his help, I removed the night guards and managed to come to you."

Nar-Narayan replied, "Bouthakrun, I had lost a sister when I was very young. Today, I feel that the almighty has bestowed upon me the return of my dear sister in you!"

Lakshmi Devi's brimming eyes couldn't control her tears anymore. She wept like a child and her beautiful lotus-like face became crimson in distress. She hesitated a bit and then said, "Brother, I cannot gather enough courage from within, but still, I am requesting you—considering me as your sister, please try to keep it. Promise me that you shall not contemplate any harm to my father-in-law for whatever he has done to you. You shall not take revenge upon him!"

Nar-Narayan paused a bit and said, "Bouthakrun, you have given me a new life. I promise you, as long as you are alive, I shall never think of harming your father-in-law."

Before leaving, he asked once again, "Bouthakrun, would you be able to reach back safely?"

Lakshmi Devi replied with a smile, "Don't worry, my brother. I will go back safely. Now hurry up!"

Nar-Narayan Ray jumped into the water through the coagulated darkness of the night and then disappeared.

---

[8] Sister-in-law

The flames of the earthen lamp in Lakshmi Devi's hands had snuffed out long ago. In the dark, she cautiously walked back toward the fortress. At a distance, she saw two gunboats of her father-in-law's fleet getting ready amid the lights from numerous burning torches.

She shuddered in fear with the thought, *'Did they find out about what I have just done?'*

With quicker steps, she reached the mouth of the secret tunnel and saw that entrance was still unhindered. Swiftly, she slipped inside the dark tunnel.

Kirti Ray believed that a rotten finger, even if it was part of oneself, needed to be cut off. Despite the pain, it was for the good of the entire body . . .

The next morning, the sun came up and illuminated the earth. But nobody ever saw Lakshmi Devi again. That night, the fierce and ruthless darkness had consumed her forever.

Nar-Narayan sat in his kingdom and learned everything. To murder his daughter-in-law, the evil Kirti Ray had sealed the secret tunnel to choke Lakshmi Devi inside that dark deathly hollow. Nar-Narayan sat speechless as he heard about the death of his beloved Bouthakrun.

A few days later, another news arrived. Kirti Ray was getting Chanchal Ray remarried with the daughter of Lakshman Ray, the zamindar of Bandura. The entire arrangement was a shrewd political allegiance. That evening, as he restlessly paced across the open rooftop of his palace in the smooth soft moonlight, Nar-Narayan Ray's eyes became moist, and his heart bled with pain. It felt as if the entire universe was getting overwhelmed by the heart-wrenching wails of despair that were emanating from Lakshmi Devi's loving soul. It seemed as though her radiant smile was reflecting upon the entire earth, over the vast woodlands, and was lending an ethereal beauty to the pure moonlight scattered across the world. It appeared that the beautiful aura of her eyes was sparkling across the stars. Sadly, she wasn't there to console her brother anymore.

Nar-Narayan Ray's ancestors were bold and fearless bandits. In that moment of supreme anger, the blood of his barbaric ancestors started to flood his veins. Nar-Narayan vowed, "Bouthakrun, I forgot my own dishonor, but I shall not forgive them for the injustice they have done to you. Those criminals have murdered you mercilessly. I must avenge your death!"

A few days later, on a cold winter morning, Kirti Ray saw that the entrance of the moat around his fortress was crowded with warships, longboats, and gunboats of a huge naval force. The explosions of cracking cannons were shaking the very foundation of his entire palace. News arrived quickly and he was shocked to hear that Nar-Narayan Ray had declared war. With him was Portuguese pirate, Sebastião Gonzales. A part of their combined naval forces, comprising of forty war vessels, attacked Kirti Ray's fortress at the mouth of the creek, while the rest of it were waiting in the main river in anticipation of their turn to assault.

Kirti Ray was prepared for such unpredicted attacks, but he was not prepared for the collaborative assault of Sebastião Gonzales and Nar-Narayan Ray. For years, Gonzales was in constant battle with Ramchandra Ray, and Kirti Ray didn't expect in his wildest dreams that a coalition could be formed between a leaseholder under Ramchandra Ray and Gonzales. However, the wicked zamindar was unnerved by the sudden assault. He was not a man who would be grounded so easily. Hence, canons started to rage out from his fortress to retaliate against the enemy's attack.

Ten gunboats, from the skillful naval force of Gonzales, went behind the sandbars and tried to enter the smaller creek adjacent to the moat. But Kirti Ray's navy apprehended them with heavy shelling; Gonzales realized that they wouldn't be able to withstand such severe confrontation for long. He left two of his gunboats at that place, took the rest away, and parked them behind the sandbars. Then, his trusted aide, another fearsome pirate named Michael Rosario de Vega, took a smaller fleet and entered the moat to attack the fortress from the west.

The unexpected attack from all sides blocked Kirti Ray's naval fleet inside the moat as if it was stuck inside a corked bottle. They failed to get out into the main river and retaliate against the enemy's fleet. Kirti Ray's own naval fleet wasn't a weak one, but it struggled to tackle the attack from all sides.

By evening, under the continuous shelling from Rosario's fleet of gunboats, the western side of the fortress rumbled and broke down. The entire portion fell off like a pack of straws. A shocked Kirti Ray saw that the ruins of thirty shattered warships of his own fleet were floating near the mouth of the creek. No more canons were being fired from the fortress. The glaring guns of his forces had fallen silent. Across the horizon, along the banks of the big river, the evening was drawing down its dark curtain. A pack of vultures was flying in circles in the sky above the wrecked fortress. It was a clear summon of the ghastly bloodbath and his brutal defeat.

Suddenly, the face of Lakshmi Devi flashed across Nar-Narayan Ray's eyes. Her faint distressed expression and frightened tearful eyes were overflowing with sorrow. In deep remorse, he repented, "Oh, what have I done? Is this how I have kept the promise that I made to my sister? Is this how I have honored her last request?"

Nar-Narayan screamed out and commanded, "No one in Kirti Ray's family must die!"

However, after a while, it was revealed that the palace was completely empty. Surprisingly, it was completely abandoned, and all its inhabitants seemed to have disappeared. A stunned Nar-Narayan rushed inside the fortress to verify that strange news. Gonzales and Nar-Narayan combed every corner of that wrecked fort and discovered that it was indeed completely empty. The Portuguese pirates entered the castle to ransack it, but they found absolutely no valuables. The plunder went on until the next afternoon, but no one in Kirti Ray's family could be found. In the evening, Nar-Narayan Ray left two gunboats behind as sentinels before making his way back.

A few more days passed, and the Portuguese pirates finished looting the fort. Then, one day, a servant of Kirti Ray entered the ruins. On the morning of that fateful attack, he had run away from the palace. He returned when the battle ended. As he roamed around, he reached a broken pillar and stopped in surprise. Behind the pillar, he saw a man fatally injured on the floor. As the servant went near, he recognized him. The latter was one of the most trusted aides to Kirti Ray.

The injured man was trying hard to say something but was unable to utter any words. From those faint and broken words of the dying man, the servant deciphered a meaning that made him thunderstruck. In a shuddering angst, he stood there and sweated profusely. He learned that Kirti Ray had taken shelter inside a secret chamber of that fort. With him were his family and all the wealth that he had garnered. The dying man was the only one who knew about the location of that chamber.

In those days, almost every fort had secret chambers. Such chambers usually had a peculiar design system. Entrances to those secret chambers could only be opened from outside. Anybody hiding inside the secret chambers had to depend on a trusted aide to open the door to let them out.

Before the injured man could reveal the location of that secret chamber, he died. Hence, the location of that chamber inside some hidden dark tunnel remained elusive forever! Unfortunately, Kirti Ray and his family were trapped inside that deathly hollow.

One by one, they witnessed their approaching deaths as they suffered from hunger, thirst, fear, and agony. Then, in the absence of fresh air, the ill-fated family of Kirti Ray choked to death. Nobody could ever discover the location of that secret chamber. Under the ruins of the colossal castle, their rotten bones disintegrated to dust in that dark, deathly hollow. No one could find them ever . . .

*

That day, I came to know about the strange and uncanny fable that still exists in those waters . . .

The narrow creek was a tributary of Sandwip Channel. At a distance, inside the dense woods, the remnant ruins of Kirti Ray's fort, perhaps, exist to this day. It was called the fateful Gor of Kirti Pasha. Close to the bank of the creek, a cluster of old bullet-wood trees stood like ghosts amid an impenetrable forest of thorns and wild foliage. Not far off, a large lake comes into sight. On its south, wrecks of broken brick structures resembling huge, decorated shark heads and decaying pillars still reflect the faint rays of the past glory of the Bengal of the Baro-Bhuiyans. The staircase leading to that lake, on which the footsteps of the queens once created a magical aura, has become the abode of wild tigers who come to drink water from it. Poisonous snakes roam freely across those ancient relics.

During nights, when the forests become silent, when the mangrove trees stand tall like dark apparitions, when the salty water of the bay nears the creek during high tide and glows like a bunch of fireflies at the mouth of the creek . . . many passing sailors, boatmen, and wild-honey collectors have heard the otherworldly shrieks not once but many times.

The unnerving shrieks pierce through the dark night's sheath across the vast wilderness, like some ghostly arrows of dissonance and dispersed across the sky.

Ohh, you who have come, Ohh, passing traveler . . . Take us out of this hell. Oh, passing boatmen and sailors . . . come and save us! Please save us . . .

In the terror of those paranormal wails, nobody dares to sail across those waters during the night.

***

A Paranormal Illusion

It happened two years ago. Bits and pieces of that incident still come back to my mind like gushes of wild breeze. How did I come here? What happened thereafter?

Let me bring back those obscure memories and relive that story once again, bit by bit . . .

The long road meandered from Bagula toward Seedhrani. Perhaps, it was always there, and I started walking along it. I, a Brahmin by caste and a servant by occupation, was content with my job as a domestic cook, but that day I lost my job. I wasn't unhappy to lose the job that I had been diligently performing for years. I was unhappy because I was laid off unjustly. No, I didn't steal ghee from my masters' kitchen; I was a loyal servant. And no, I didn't know who stole it. However, my masters made their decision and declared me the culprit. Hence, I ended up jobless and became a stranded man with no work and nowhere to live. And thus, my vagabond journey began. I hardly knew what was destined for me.

As I crossed the villages of Shantipara, Shorshe, and Bejerdanga, it was well past noontime. I walked for a long, and my famished stomach began to torment my senses with hunger pangs. I was young, and I had some money with me that I had saved. However, in that vast rural landscape, the sight of even a dilapidated eatery was like a distant dream.

Suddenly, I noticed something. Along the path, there was a beautiful pond. The fresh water of that pond sparkled in the sunlight, a sight that attracted me to the core. I walked down the broken flight of steps, undressed myself, and descended into the water. I removed the overgrowth of water hyacinth and floating vegetation and dove across the cool water. It was the end of *Baisakh*[9] month, and summer was hot and humid. The swim in that freshwater pond rejuvenated my mind and soul. However, even as my body had cooled down with respite, the fire in my stomach had magnified. To satiate my hunger, I looked around in the adjacent woods. Even wild fruit would have been sufficient to help me satisfy my hunger for some time. Unfortunately, I couldn't find anything edible anywhere.

Suddenly, I noticed an old man. He was coming toward the pond, perhaps to take a bath. As he came nearer, he noticed me and asked, "Where are you from?"

I replied, "Babu, I am a poor Brahmin, and I am in search of a job. But right now, I am very hungry, and I desperately need some food. Can you please tell me where I can get some for myself?"

The old man looked at me and said, "Be patient. Let me take my bath, and then I will make the necessary arrangements."

The old man took his bath, got dressed, and then took me along. We went into the nearby village and then he took me inside

---

[9] Baisakh is the first month in the twelve months of the Bengali calendar. It also marks the beginning of the new year in Bengal.

an empty house that was surrounded by a thicket of shrubbery. The house was located on the outskirts of the village and was adjacent to the dense woods.

As we went inside, the old man said, "My name is Nibaran Chakraborty, and this is my house. However, I don't live here anymore. My sons have their own businesses in Kolkata, and they live with their families in the Shyam bazaar locality. So, we have left behind this sprawling house and now live in the city by managing ourselves within the three miniscule rooms in a rented apartment."

The man looked sad, and he said in a regretful voice, "Isn't it such a shame? I come here once every month to take care of my beloved house. My sons fear malaria, so they avoid visiting this place. Hence, I often come here alone. There is a huge garden behind this house teemed with abundant vegetation. Numerous plants and trees bear plethora of fruits and vegetables. Sadly, in our absence, this neglected bounty of natural is being enjoyed by strangers!"

He paused a bit and then asked, "Would you like to stay here?"

I asked eagerly, "What work shall I have?"

"Well, you can be the resident cook in this house," the old man replied, "Till the time I am here, you can cook for both of us and stay here with me. Then, when I go back to the city, you can live here and take care of my beloved house."

"That's great. I accept the offer," I replied happily.

As I agreed to his proposal, the old man became extremely happy and quickly arranged some food for me. Then, he gave me an old mattress and some pillows and said, "Now go and take some rest."

The long journey had left me exhausted, so I quickly fell asleep. When I woke up, daylight had started to fade, and the evening's sheath had started to draw its dark curtain all around us. Careless touches of the evening twilight's crimson hue lingered along the tall trees, and the distant howls of wild wolves reverberated through the nearby forests.

That evening, I went out of the house and roamed around for some time. All around the village were wild woods of mango or jackfruit trees. The woods were dense, and I couldn't find any houses nearby. Old Nibaran Chakraborty's house was indeed situated far from the village's prime localities.

As I walked, I noticed a dilapidated wall around the house. It was like a ramshackle boundary of brick and mortar. I peeped through one of the holes in that wall and saw Nibaran Chakraborty siting in his courtyard, quietly smoking his hookah.

As the evening deepened, I went back to the house. Nibaran Chakraborty asked me to make some tea and roast some *chira*[10]. He smirked and said, "Hot tea, along with freshly roasted chira mixed with mustard oil and salt is an excellent snack! We can savor it with fresh green chilies from my garden."

I followed his instructions and the two of us had a quiet evening over tea. Then, an hour later, he asked me, "Prepare the rice for boiling. There is a stock of thin fragmented rice in the granary. With boiled potatoes and some fresh ghee, it would make a hearty dinner for you and me."

I obeyed his request and started the preparations. He added, "There are ample ridge gourd plants in the garden behind the kitchen. Make curry for yourself with them. It is not yet late at the night. Take a lantern and go to the garden to fetch some ridge gourd for yourself. And one more thing, always keep the kitchen illuminated. Never leave it in the dark."

I felt surprised and replied, "Yes Babu, that is necessary. Or else, how will I cook?"

"Yes . . . yes, that is what I meant," murmured the old man.

---

[10] Flattened rice.

Nibaran Chakraborty's house was indeed a huge one. Spread across two floors, it probably had fourteen or fifteen rooms. In front of the kitchen was a sprawling porch. At its corner, there was a cluster of coconut trees and one pomelo tree. To pluck the ridge gourd, I had to walk across the porch, enter the courtyard, and then go around it to reach the backyard behind the kitchen.

The fading twilight hadn't dissolved completely, and I thought, *'I don't need to carry a lantern. Things are still somewhat visible, and I shall quickly collect the ridge gourd and come back.'*

As I went inside the garden, I realized that it was a dense wood of unkempt shrubbery. A vast overgrowth of the wild ridge gourd plants had almost covered the entire area. Amid that abundance of ridge gourd, I started to collect the newer and fresher ones.

All of a sudden, I noticed something. At about a couple of yards, I saw a woman. In that obscured visibility of the evening, I could see her outline. Her veil was pulled down across her face and she was kneeling to pick a ridge gourd. I stood there and observed for a while. It felt a bit awkward, so I focused back on my work, and then, before returning, I turned once more and saw that she was still busy plucking ridge gourds.

When I went back inside the house, Nibaran Chakraborty asked, "Could you find the ridge gourds?"

"Yes, I did," I replied, "your garden has an ample supply of ridge gourds. However, there was someone else too who was plucking them."

The old man was astonished and asked, "Where?"

"Behind the kitchen, in the backyard garden where the shrubbery is denser," I replied.

"Was it a man?" he asked.

"No, it was a woman," I answered. "Probably a housewife from the village."

Nibaran Chakraborty became skeptical and said, "Where is she? Let's go and see. Show me where you saw her."

I accompanied him and went back to the place behind the kitchen's backyard where I had seen that woman. But as we reached the garden, there was nobody to be seen! The woman had vanished, and the place was empty.

"Where is the woman?" asked the old man.

"Over there . . ." I said quickly, "she was near those bushes. But she is gone now."

Nibaran Chakraborty said in a sarcastic tone, "Ah . . . mister cook, let's go back. I guess you were daydreaming about the woman!"

I was surprised. I thought . . . *Why is the old man so finicky about it? What is the problem if a woman had come to pluck some ridge gourd from this neglected garden? Moreover, it is a sheer coincidence that he is here in his house tonight. On days when he lives in the city, who guards the ridge gourds in his beloved garden?'*

After dinner, old Nibaran Chakraborty again picked up the topic. He said, "Why didn't you take a lantern with you? Didn't I ask you to do so? Why didn't you do that?"

I couldn't understand what the entire problem was. What wrong did I do? I concluded that Nibaran Chakraborty was a very fussy old man. Or else, why would anybody be so concerned about such a trivial matter? Why would one carry a lantern when the surroundings were still visible?

The old man again warned me, "After the evening, wherever you go, always carry a light with you, even if visibility is not completely obscured."

"Why so?" I asked skeptically.

"Young man, how old are you?" asked Nibaran Chakraborty.

"Around twenty-seven or thirty years," I replied.

"That is why you need to listen to me," said my new master. "You are much younger than me. I am sixty-three. Listen carefully to whatever I say."

Without further argument, I agreed and said humbly, "Yes, Babu. I will follow your words."

That night, as I went to bed, my sleep was disrupted by a strange mechanical sound. It was coming from the room just above the one in which I was sleeping. I became alert and tried to listen carefully. The sounds were indeed real. It was as though somebody was trying to drag some heavy furniture across the room. It seemed as if someone or a few people were moving their furniture from one side of the room to the other.

I wondered . . . *Perhaps, old Nibaran Chakraborty is packing his stuff. He is supposed to go back to Kolkata tomorrow, so maybe he is finishing his packing. But why is he doing that so late in the night? Oh, he really is strange and crazily finicky.'*

The next morning, I asked him about the incident, and he replied, "Who, me?"

I said, "Yes. Weren't you packing your stuff upstairs in the middle of the night?"

Nibaran Chakraborty replied nervously, "Yeah . . . yes. Well, no. Ah, correct."

"Babu, you could've asked me to do the packing", I said, "I would've done it happily for you. You didn't have to take all the trouble and that too so late in the night."

The old man listened to me and became quiet. He didn't say anything further and sat silently.

By nine o'clock in the morning I finished cooking some rice and pulses and fried some ridge gourd. Nibaran Chakraborty finished his meal and then picked up his luggage to leave. However, before leaving, he pleaded to me, "Stay in this house as if it is your own. Young Brahmin, don't treat yourself as a resident cook. Consider this place your own house. Fruits and vegetables are abundant in my garden. Treat yourself to the excess of guavas, mangoes, papayas, and jackfruits in those trees. In your leisure time, plant good vegetables in the fertile soil and enjoy the yield. Eat whatever you can and sell the rest. This is now your own house. Take care of it and live here without any inhibitions or worries. And one more thing . . ."

"What is it?" I asked.

Nibaran Chakraborty lowered his voice and said, "There would be many who would come to disturb you. They would try to misguide you. They would try to poison your mind and try to split your judgments. Don't listen to those fools. This is a golden opportunity for you. Take care of my house. Stay here happily on your own. Don't listen to any of the gossip or unnecessary chatter. Enjoy the rich vegetation in the garden and live happily. I have opened two rooms for you. Don't listen to anybody and stay without any worries."

And then, old Nibaran Chakraborty went away. He left me in the lap of opulence. For a poor, homeless Brahmin like me, it felt like I was atop the clouds! Inside the enormous house, I had two huge rooms just for my personal use. Apart from that, the veranda, the kitchen, the porch, and the courtyard . . . everything was mine to use. There was a nice draw-well to fetch fresh water too. I could hardly believe the grace of my luck.

The old man gave me ten rupees in advance and left behind half a maund of fine rice. With the plentiful harvest of fruits and vegetables from the garden, it was like an unexpected God's gift to me!

In the afternoon, I went out to find a local grocery shop. Old Nibaran Chakraborty's house was surrounded by dense woods, and I struggled my way out through them. The house was located at a remote corner of the village with no trace of any habitation nearby. I traversed down the thin rustic path and walked half a mile to reach the neighborhood inside the village. As I went, I met a man on my way. He too was going toward a grocery store. He asked me, "Where do you live?"

I replied, "I am staying at Nibaran Chakraborty's house on the outskirts of this village."

The man raised his eyebrows in astonishment and said, "Nibaran Chakraborty's house? But why?"

"I am the new caretaker of the house," I said, "I just came here yesterday."

"Nobody can stay in that house. You too won't be able to stay there," the man whispered in a cautious voice.

"Why is that?" I asked in a surprised voice.

"Mark my words. You shall soon know if I am telling the truth or not," replied the man in a mysterious tone. "Many had come to that house and many had gone. But no one could persist. Even Nibaran Chakraborty's own family was unable to live in that house. Don't you see? His sons and daughters-in-laws never even visit that cursed house!"

I became more skeptical and asked, "But why?"

"I don't know," he said, "that is a mysteriously dangerous house. The villagers believe that it is cursed. You are a stranger in this village. Be very careful."

Without wasting any more time, the man quickly hurried away. I found a local grocery store, bought a few items, and went back. The man left me in a state of disbelief. As I was returning, I could see the house in the evening twilight. I could see the huge house of Nibaran Chakraborty standing tall like an apparition amid the woods. The monstrous structure left a sudden touch of fear in my heart. It looked like a living creature of brick and mortar with a sinister frown. It seemed it was capable of consuming insignificant mortals like me in a single gulp.

As I walked toward the house, it looked as if it was coming closer and closer to catch and consume me as its prey. Why did it suddenly appear like that? I don't really know . . .

I consoled myself and thought, *'It is just a bad imagination. That strange man left an unnecessary doubt in my heart. He is the one who is responsible for poisoning my mind with superstition. I was so happy when I headed out to find the grocery store, but that man came suddenly and planted the seeds of suspicion with his weird stories. Why did he have to come so proactively and tell me all that rubbish? Old Nibaran Chakraborty had warned me of such people from the village. He cautioned me not to listen to their gibberish. They are jealous of my sudden prosperity and good luck.'*

My mind told my heart, *'Don't worry. The sly villagers steal freely from the fertile and abundant garden of Nibaran Chakraborty. My arrival in the house as a vigilant caretaker creates a hindrance to their unobstructed intrusions. That is why they are trying to scare me away. That woman I saw last evening must have had a similar intention.'*

It had been days since I had experienced such luxury. It was a golden opportunity to earn money without any effort. The only work I had was to cook for myself. That's it. I began to enjoy my life with the unexpected gift of God. Every morning, I had to cook my food and then I could relax on the huge porch or in the courtyard. I could sing along on my own without anybody giving me any instructions. In that relentless freedom, I could do anything I wanted.

One evening, something astounding happened. Water started to flow through the drainpipe from the upper floor, as if somebody was washing their hands and feet in the veranda. The flow of water was quite strong, and I was left astonished. How was it possible? I went and stood at a corner of the porch and tried to look at the veranda. The flow of water through the drainpipe was significant. It was an impossible occurrence. Given that nobody lived upstairs, it was a bizarre affair that had no explanation. How was the water coming through the drainpipe?

The water stopped flowing after ten minutes. Fueled by my curiosity, I reasoned, "Maybe old Nibaran Chakraborty had left a pitcher upstairs and it happened to topple. That'd be the only plausible explanation. I was simply overthinking. Otherwise, from where the water would come?"

An hour later, I went to bed. I extinguished the lamp, closed my eyes, and almost immediately, fell asleep. Much later in the night, my sleep was broken and I sat up. The serene white hue of the moonlight was soaking the entire room. A fragrance of an unknown bloom filled the air with its sweetness. It felt a bit odd. Ever since my arrival, I hadn't noticed any fragrant flower plants around the house. Then, where was the scent coming from?

Suddenly, a chill ran down my spine and I jumped up on the bed. Did I just see a woman walk past the window of my room? Yes, I was sure about it. There was no doubt. A woman had quickly walked past the open window, and I saw her clearly.

I got off my bed, opened the door, and ran outside into the porch. As I stood flabbergasted, I realized two things: first, the intensity of the floral fragrance was now less than before. And second, it was probably the woman who was responsible for spreading that sweet fragrance.

No, it was not the fragrance of any flower. I was unable to recognize the fragrance. It started to make me feel dizzy.

In a state of trance, questions started to fill my mind ... *Why did I come out? What am I doing on the porch? That mysterious woman who had spread this intoxicating fragrance is nowhere to be seen. Where is she? Where did she vanish?'*

With no clue about what was happening, I went back inside my room. I was still in a state of shock, and I fell on my bed. Then, I fell asleep.

The next morning, as I woke up, the bright sunlight lifted my mood. With positive confidence, I said to myself, "It was just a wild dream!"

Leaving aside all worries, I focused on my work. At first, I contemplated a plan to clear out the overgrowth in the garden and planned to plant different vegetables in the fertile soil. The only discomfort was that the house was completely secluded from the rest of the village. The lonely existence was the sole unbearable factor to living in that house. Only if there were even a couple of households nearby, then it wouldn't have felt so desolate. There was no one with whom I could even speak for a moment. That was the biggest and the only agony.

That afternoon, something happened again. I had just finished cooking a meal for myself and was taking the utensils down from the clay stove when I sat frozen with fear by a sudden gust of roaring laughter that came from upstairs. It seemed that a group of people roared with laughter with a terrible intensity that stopped the entire universe and frightened me to the core. The surreal reverberations of those supernatural laughs shook my entire body in their eerie rhythm and cacophonic pitches.

I left behind everything and ran outside. As I reached the porch and looked up, I couldn't see anybody. The doors and windows on the upper floor were shut and locked, just like they had been ever since I came. The eerily echoing laughter came to a sudden stop, and everything became completely silent. It was a bizarre moment of shock and the silence felt unbearable. How was that possible? Who was laughing madly and then stopped with such abruptness? I couldn't decipher any meaning from it.

As my nerves calmed down, I thought, *What is the matter? In this secluded house, have a gang of notorious men made their secret den upstairs?*

I went near the stairways and checked everything closely. The door in front of the stairs was still locked tightly. There was no sign of any trespassing. I didn't feel afraid of the paranormal. In the bright daylight, such ghostly thoughts don't disturb the mind of a sane human being. So, I didn't experience it too. However, I am sure, if the incident had happened at night, I would have become unnerved. Such was the unexpectedness of that mysterious episode.

I came back to the kitchen and focused on my work. I cooked some ridge gourd curry that I could eat with the rice I had just prepared. With an abundance of ridge gourd in Nibaran Chakraborty's garden, it almost became a staple for my daily diet. Well, it was *my* garden now. Despite being a mere servant, I was the indisputable lord of that enormous house and the huge adjacent garden. In the absence of any owner, everything belonged to me and no one was there to question my deeds. The feeling of ownership had a strange intoxication that made me ecstatic. For a poor man like me, it was a life of dreams!

As I prepared my meal, I remained cautious and tried to hear any sound that might come from upstairs. But not even the sound of a pin dropping down on the floor could be heard. Finally, I gave up. Then, I had my lunch and went to sleep. But that was not the end of the ordeal. Perhaps, the ordeal had just begun . . .

As I fell asleep, it felt as if I was lying inside a room that was packed with people who were talking loudly with each other. It felt as though I was inside a room filled with guests who were attending a wedding and were talking heartily with each other. I was again in a semi-conscious state where I could feel the presence of those people, but they all seemed so very vaporous.

I thought . . . *'All this is the outcome of my wild imagination. This is also a hallucination, just like the laughter that I had heard.'*

*

Nine more days passed, and they went without any disturbances.

It is a natural human tendency to forget unpleasant incidents. We quickly forget the trauma of adverse experiences because the human heart always tries to eliminate negative thoughts. So, I started telling myself, *'It was nothing! I must have been hallucinating. My eyes were misled by an imaginary sight of that woman and my ears were tricked by the illusory sounds that were nonexistent. Ah . . . . I was grossly mistaken by a bogus fear.'*

Within those few days, my health improved drastically. In the absence of any work throughout the day, I just ate and slept without any worries. A kind of lethargy grasped me. I had always been an active individual. I never liked to remain idle for long. However, inside that house, strange inertia overwhelmed my entire being. My heart only desired to stay idle. I just wanted to rest and do absolutely nothing. Perhaps, I was too tired due to years of hard work and my lethargy was a result of that extreme exhaustion. I don't know the exact reason behind it, but I just wanted to stop doing anything and relax boundlessly.

On the ninth day, as the evening twilight was approaching as a harbinger of the night, I thought, "Perhaps, I should clear out the overgrowth around the ridge gourd bushes and make space to plant some taro roots. The soil behind the kitchen is fertile and I must utilize it. I have also seen a tender vine of ash gourd in the garden. I shall put it atop the roof of the kitchen with the help of a stick. It'd be easier to perform this task as the owner has meticulously stocked a variety of gardening tools like spades, choppers, cleavers, and axes."

I went out with the tools and began my work in the garden. The sunlight was fading fast, but the visibility wasn't obscured yet. I sat down and focused on my work. About half an hour later, I lifted my head and was surprised to see that a woman was kneeling near some adjacent bushes, busy plucking some ridge gourds. Almost instantaneously, an uproar of human voices reverberated across the upper floor of the house. It seemed as though about fifty people were creating a hullabaloo! In that eerie commotion, all the doors and windows on the first floor flung open together.

In a state of total shock, I left everything behind and ran toward the house. As I reached the porch, I looked up to see what was happening. But once again to my sheer surprise, I saw that everything was normal. Every door and window on the first floor was shut as usual, and there was total silence all around.

I didn't know what was going on. I stood there speechless and speculated, "What is the matter? Is this house epileptic? Does it suddenly break out in some supernatural fit of cries? No, this time, I am not mistaken. I was working diligently in the garden, and I was in a completely sane state when I heard that creepy uproar. Now, when I am standing here, everything again is eerily silent, as if nothing happened What is going on?"

Suddenly, I remembered something . . . That woman! Yes, amid this turmoil, that mysterious woman had again come to collect ridge gourds in the garden behind the kitchen. Without wasting any time, I ran and reached the place where I had spotted her a few moments ago. Unfortunately, she was gone too! She had vanished and the place was deserted.

Within the strange household of Nibaran Chakraborty, I was amid an inexplicable drama of eeriness that had an uncanny amusement buried in it.

That night, something happened . . . something that was, once again, creepily amusing . . .

I finished my dinner and went to bed. While I remained in a state of semi-consciousness, my sleep failed to deepen significantly, until a sudden shock pulled me back to full awareness. I opened my eyes and was horrified to see that I was not alone in the room. I was surrounded by a huge mob who crowded the entire room and around my bed. Every one of them wore a red colored turban and each of them carried a small stick in their hands. As if this wasn't enough, the faces of those men were identical, too! It was a surreal sight, and a cold chill ran down my spine. In that unnerving instance, I was shocked to realize that I was amid fifty absolutely identical men.

One of them, amid that eerie crowd, said, "Today, someone new has arrived amidst us!"

Another of them replied, "For a long time, a mortal human being's house has been existing in this place. I haven't seen that house. I have only heard about it from those amongst us who had seen it. There is a man, a human being, who now lives in that house."

The first voice answered, "It is a lie! Where is that house?"

A third voice added, "No. None of us have seen it."

The first voice said aloud, "Then come, let us begin our dance!"

And then began an enactment of eccentricity as the vaporous creatures, those identical men, pranced and swirled across the room while a few of them grouped to beat their equally surreal drums. The entire room seemed to reverberate in the cacophony of their screams and roars while I sat speechless and witnessed that inexplicable supernatural phenomenon. Their sublime bodies passed through my own body as if I was thin air! Nothing touched me or my bed. It seemed like I was a non-existent entity, and those paranormal creatures were completely unaware of my presence. They were completely oblivious to the unbearable discomfort and horror that I was experiencing.

The shock of witnessing their ghostly revelry, singing, and dancing was too big for my nerves to tolerate for long. Hence, being terrified to the core, I fell unconscious.

It was long past midnight when I regained consciousness. I opened my eyes and saw that a soft moonshine had flooded the entire room. That mysteriously familiar floral fragrance was smeared in the cool breeze that was floating inside. In that partly

78

conscious state, I looked outside the window toward the moonlit-washed woods. Perhaps, the serene softness of the sight calmed my nerves, and I kept staring at it.

I don't remember how long I was in that condition, but soon I fell asleep. Eventually, the dawn broke and ushered in the fresh sunlight. When I woke up, I realized something strange. My body and my mind were both completely rejuvenated just one feels after a fresh and deep sleep. I wondered why I was not feeling tired, given that I had experienced a bizarre pandemonium that was bound to give me a disturbed sleep. However, inexplicably, I was feeling completely invigorated.

Once again, I wondered, "Wasn't it me who saw that paranormal revelry of ghosts who were dancing all around me? Or was it a sheer dream? Well, if it was truly a dream, then where did that mysterious floral fragrance come from? Whenever that shadowy woman comes out for her nocturnal walk and strolls past the window, that overwhelming fragrance intoxicates me. I experienced that fragrance last night too. No, I am not wrong. It was real. The remnant of that intoxicating fragrance is still fresh in my senses. Is it really a paranormal phenomenon or the fragrance of some unknown wildflower? Maybe, the latter is the truth that explains it."

That afternoon, I went to the grocery store to fetch some cooking oil. The grocer recognized me and asked, "Hey, how are you? Have you seen anything in that house?"

In an unimaginable mechanical state, I replied automatically, "No."

"Didn't you hear anything?" he asked with surprise.

Once more, I replied automatically, "No."

He sighed relief and said, "You have been saved. Before you came, two others had tried to live in that cursed house and both had seen a creepy woman. They saw that mysterious woman almost every night. Then, a deadly insanity gripped them. Finally, they became unwilling to even step out of that abominable house. They both soon died."

He paused and said, "That house is an abode of ghosts. Those creepy creatures drive human beings to lunacy! Any wretched human who chooses to live in that house remains sleepless inside that fatal abyss and starves to death . . . I guess you know the spells to keep those horrible creatures away. We, the villagers, don't even dare pass by that vexatious house."

Without further discussion, I bought the cooking oil and came back. A thought kept lingering in my mind . . . *Have I started to become a lunatic too?* However, as soon as I stepped inside the house, my mind told me . . . '*No. It's all a lie! I am so happy inside this house. Am I not? Where else will I go leaving behind such luxury? This existence is the best that I can ever expect. It is an ethereal gift . . .*'

*

It has been two years since that fateful night. I still live in that house; I am the sole resident. Neither Nibaran Chakraborty pays me, nor does he come to visit his beloved house. But that is absolutely fine. I am happy with my own bizarre existence. I take care of this house. I grow my own yield in the fertile garden. I eat whatever I can and sell the rest. At night, I witness the paranormal revelry . . . every night, I become a spectator of the ghostly being with whom I have a mutual coexistence now. But I don't dare to leave this beloved house. It is my house!

Were those bizarre creatures of the otherworld? Was the house a place where the universe of the living and the universe of the dead existed in parallel?

Perhaps, the answers to these questions do not exist.

***

Curious Case of the Paranormal Medal

My name is Suren and this peculiar incident happened four long years ago. Now that I remember it, everything seems like a complete myth. Perhaps, I was indisposed; I must have hallucinated the whole episode. It was probably the result of my own imagination that my fatigued mind had seen that illusion. Strangely, even to this day, my heart continues to disagree with my mind. It refuses to accept the logic that the mind tries to weave. It believes that there is no reason why I should reject that curious incident as a mere piece of my own imagination. It strongly believes that my bizarre experience was a harsh reality. Whatever my mind is contemplating now, that is untrue.

Let me reveal the story in detail . . .

Before I continue, let me divulge that throughout the entire last decade, I had never been afflicted with any disease. My mind and my heart are both completely healthy, and were so even at the time when that incident took place.

My life as a schoolmaster had always been a regular and ordinary one. I never faced or saw anything that I could depict as extraordinary. Just like the regular life of any other schoolmaster, mine too followed a monotonous routine of duties over the years.

During the monsoon season that year, just after summer vacation had ended, I was teaching in the classroom when a quarrel broke out between two students. One of them was trying to snatch away something from the other while the latter resisted with full power.

I raised my voice and scolded them, when another boy said aloud, "Sir, Kamakhyacharan is trying to snatch Sudhir's medal."

In an alarmed and angry voice, I asked, "Whose medal? What medal?"

Kamakhyacharan protested, "No sir, I wasn't snatching it. I just wanted to take a look, so I asked for it. But he denied."

I replied, "The medal belongs to him. If he is unwilling to share it, then you don't have the right to snatch it away. Sit down and do not do such a thing again."

Thereafter, I delivered a brief lecture on mutual harmony and brotherhood, and then asked, "Sudhir, where is the medal? Where did you get it from?"

In my mind, I thought that perhaps Sudhir had participated in some sports activities that usually take place in local clubs around Kolkata and might have earned a coin-sized medal for his participation. It was quite usual that the young boy had brought it to school to flaunt it in front of his fellow classmates. In my wild imagination, I even visualized that the students were probably planning to meet the headmaster and appeal for an early leave to celebrate his momentous triumph. So when the medal reached my hands, I took it with contempt.

However, when I looked at it, I felt a sudden alertness. It was not an ordinary medal. It was an antique! The item was quite large and had an excellent finish. Deep down, I felt curious to take a closer look at it. There were some words engraved on the medal, but the lack of adequate illumination made it difficult for me to read them. On the opposite side, a small depiction of Queen Victoria was neatly engraved.

Meanwhile, a small crowd of curious students gathered around me. I scolded them and said, "Go back to your seats. I don't want my students to swarm around like this inside the classroom."

I called one of the boys and asked, "Can you read what is written here?"

The young boy struggled a bit and read out slowly, "C-r-i-m-e-a . . . Sevastopol . . . Victoria R-e-g-i-n-a."

"Now read what is written on the opposite side," I said with an invigorated enthusiasm.

He read out, "Sergeant S.B. Parkins, 6th Dragon Guards, Year 1854."

The revelation formally made me speechless. The object dated back to the era of the Crimean War. It was probably awarded to someone named Sergeant Parkins, who was a soldier in the Dragon Guards regiment of England, for his valiant service in guarding Sevastopol during the war. I was left stunned! That medal was no ordinary object. It was of great historical significance.

I wondered in amazement. *'Crimea . . . Sevastopol? Charge of The Light Brigade! But how did such a thing come into the possession of little Sudhir who lived in Kolkata city's dingy Neel-Mani-Das Lane?'*

I called Sudhir to my desk and asked, "Where did you get this medal from?"

"It is mine," replied Sudhir.

"I know it's yours," I said, "but where did you get it from?"

"My grandpa gave it to me," confessed Sudhir.

I questioned, "And, where did he get it from? Do you know that?"

"Yes sir, I know," said Sudhir. "An Englishman Sahib had kept it with my grandpa's father."

"How?" I asked.

"Sir, my great-grandfather was the owner of an alcohol shop and a bar. Once, after having a few drinks at the bar, when that Englishman couldn't pay off his bill, he had mortgaged it with my great-grandfather. But he never came again to take it back. That is what my grandpa told me."

I deciphered and thought . . . *Well, it's been eighty-six years since Sergeant Parkins might have this medal. If he was even twenty years old at that time, now he would be a hundred and six years old! So, it is obvious that the man is surely dead . . .'*

As it was a Saturday, the classes were supposed to get over early. I had already planned to visit my ancestral home in the village after a long time. In my village lived an old man who, much like a neighborhood uncle to me throughout my childhood, was an expert in history. He was a well-learned man. I knew it was his hobby to study interesting historical facts. So, I decided to show him the medal. I was certain that he would be thrilled to see such an antique.

I requested to borrow the medal from Sudhir and promised to return it on the upcoming Monday. After school was over, I went back, packed my suitcase, and reached Sealdah Junction Railway Station. From there, I boarded the train at 2:30 p.m. and arrived at my village's railway station at around 5:30 p.m. Then, I walked down two long miles to finally reach my ancestral home.

It was the end of the *Bhadra*[11] month, but the monsoons had been very uneven. So, the rural roads were mostly dry. After living

---

[11] Bhadra Month, also known as Bhadra Mash, is the fifth month in the traditional Bengali calendar followed in West Bengal and some other places in Eastern India.

in the city for a prolonged period, the abundance of greenery on both sides of the road seemed even more soothing to my eyes. Thus, somewhat deliberately, I walked slowly while enjoying the visual bonanza of Mother Nature. By the time I reached my home, it was almost evening.

Well, to begin with, let me tell you that nobody lives in my ancestral home. Therefore, on occasions when I visit my house, an old aunt from the neighborhood cooks for me and takes care of my meals. My childhood friend from the village, Vrindavan, was an expatriate who had been living away from the village for many years. On that day, after my arrival, I was overjoyed when the old aunt said, "Your friend Vrindavan too came back to the village fifteen days ago."

I quickly freshened up, had my tea, and went out happily toward the riverbank to meet my old buddy. Before leaving, I opened my suitcase and took out the medal. I wanted to show it to him. As I reached the banks of the river, I saw that it was brimming, and the water had overflowed into the adjoining fields.

As I looked at the water, I stood there quietly for some time and then sat down at the corner of the riverbank. The evening's veil had already descended through the horizon across the landscape. The place where I sat was completely deserted. Only a cauldron of bats was returning to its roosts. At a distance, a portion of the riverbank had been eaten up by the tides. The remaining banks were quite high above the rapid current of the river water. After a while, I got up and started to walk along it.

While strolling along the river's side, I felt curious to look below. I went up to the farthest point and peeped. The place where I stood was quite high above the water level of the raging river. Suddenly, an eerie desire gripped me with a hypnotic magnetism.

It was a sudden irresistible desire to dive into the water. My inner soul clasped my senses and forced me with a fatal advice . . .
'I must jump. Yes, I must do it! I must jump into the choppy water!'

As I continued to stand at that corner, the dangerous desire too started to grow like an intoxicating suicidal craving. *'Let me jump! Yes, I have to jump. I must do it . . .'*

The river below was flowing with a monstrous current, but my subconscious soul was frantically pushing me toward a disastrous end. I didn't even know how to swim, and the water below was deep enough to grasp and drown me immediately. Ah . . . I was unable to control that maddening and deathly impulse to dive into that engulfing river. I strongly felt that if I stood there even for a few more moments, I would've failed to withhold that devilish yearning. I started to feel that my life was useless if I didn't jump into the river.

However, I gathered all my strength and pulled myself away from the riverbank. I realized that if I had lingered even a moment longer, I would have been powerless in resisting the urge to throw myself into the deadly river. My feet felt so heavy that I found them immovable, and I became almost paralyzed by that suicidal hunger.

As I moved away from the riverbank and started to walk toward Vrindavan's house, that eerie suicidal craving vanished magically. I was left astonished at that sudden fatal yearning that had gripped me beyond all sanity. I asked myself . . . *'How strange! What is the reason behind such a craving? Maybe I shouldn't have smoked excessively during the train ride. On top of that, I drank two-three helpings of hot tea. In the humid climate, those careless doings must have been the cause of that strange desire.'*

Soon, I reached Vrindavan's house. It is needless to say that my friend was overjoyed to meet me after such a long time. I, too, was thrilled to meet him. Time flew by as we sat together and chatted till late in the night. Loads of untold conversations had gathered in our hearts and we made full use of every moment.

It was a hot and humid day, and the discomfort had spilled over into the night too. The breeze also stopped blowing. It was a typical airless humid day in the month of Bhadra in Bengal.

Vrindavan said, "Let's go to the rooftop. Hope we will catch some breeze there. You must stay for dinner tonight. Maa has strictly instructed me to inform you."

It was a two-storied house, and we climbed up to the roof. It had a single room that belonged to Vrindavan's uncle. As we reached the roof, I noticed a bamboo scaffolding on the rear side of the house. I asked, "Vrindavan, are the masons working in the house?"

"Yes," replied Vrindavan, "Uncle's room is being repaired. Moreover, the bricks on the northern wall have started to show efflorescence and we plan to remove those. We have employed them to do the needful masonry work."

Saying so, he took me inside the room on the roof. However, as soon as I stepped upon the open roof, an eerie discomfort again started to clasp me. It was, once again, a strange but unknown discomfort. After a while, I felt thirsty, and I asked my friend for some water. Vrindavan got up and went downstairs to fetch it for me while I sat alone in that room. Then, I got up and started to stroll on the open roof. There was no one other with me, and the dark sheath of the night curtained the entire roof. I walked down to the corner, near the parapet, below which was the bamboo scaffolding.

Suddenly, a voice came from within . . . *'Why don't I jump? Yes, let me jump from here. It would be a great thing to do. No, it would be the best thing to do. I have to jump . . . Yes, why don't I do it right away?'*

The irresistible self-destructive urge grasped me!

At that very moment, Vrindavan arrived and called me, "Suren, come here. Come inside the room. I have got the water for you. Maa is sending some tea for us too."

The sudden interruption dissolved that creepy yearning, and I went back to the room. We kept gossiping for about half an hour. Meanwhile, tea and refreshments were served and we savored the food. We chatted for a few more hours and then Vrindavan again went downstairs to check the progress of the dinner arrangements.

Despite the late hour, it was still very humid, so I went out for a walk on the open roof. Once again, I reached the spot from where the bamboo scaffolding could be seen.

And once again, my subconscious devil called out to me . . . *'Now is the right time. I must not waste this golden opportunity. I should jump immediately from this place! Nobody is there on the roof. Nobody is there to stop me. This is the opportune moment, and I should not waste it . . .'*

Almost instantly, a second echoed from within . . . *'No! Don't be a fool. If you jump, then you will get shattered to death. That is suicide. Don't do it.'*

My head started to spin, and I felt helplessly lightheaded. I couldn't remain stable anymore and was unable to control my balance. I didn't know what happened thereafter. Maybe, I fainted . . .

*

I was jerked back from that shaky consciousness by Vrindavan's sudden shriek, "Oh my goodness, what are you doing?"

He pulled me up with his full strength. I was still feeling dizzy and was unable to decipher what had just happened. Vrindavan cried, "Why did you jump? Suren, you could've died, I saw that you jumped across the parapet when I came on the roof! Thank God your feet were stuck to the bamboo scaffolding. Otherwise, you would have crashed to your death! Suren, what happened to you? Why did you do that?"

"I . . . I don't know," I replied weakly. "My head started to spin, and I felt unsteady. Perhaps I fainted and fell. I don't recall anything after that . . ."

Vrindavan took me inside the room on the roof and made me lie down. Everyone concluded that the hectic train journey might have exhausted me on that hot and humid day, so I might have fainted and fell. However, I know that I didn't faint. That night, I willingly jumped from that parapet. It was the outcome of some uncontrolled and subconscious desire that drove me to such lunacy. Nonetheless, I could never recall what happened right at that moment when I took the step forward and jumped.

After resting for some time, I felt much better. But, as I turned my body, I felt something hard near my chest. I reached out into my pocket and took the thing out. With an uncanny surprise, I saw that it was Sudhir's medal. I was surprised because, till that moment, I had completely forgotten about that object. I held it in my hand for a while and then showed it to Vrindavan. He looked at the antique object closely and then showed it to everyone else in his house.

That night, I finished my dinner with Vrindavan, returned to my ancestral home, and went to sleep. Nobody else lived in that house and I was all alone. Strangely, I sensed a weird feeling that night that had gripped me from the moment I had stepped out of Vrindavan's house. Within my subconscious mind, I started to feel scared. It was an unknown fear of an unidentified apprehension. Moreover, the fear grew stronger as soon as I stepped inside my ancestral home.

Earlier, I had stayed alone in that house numerous times, but I never felt frightened. However, that night, a strange anxiety overwhelmed my mind. I tried to find the reason behind it and thought, *'No, I must admit that I am very tired. The train journey has exhausted me. When the body is worn out, the mind too gets tired. It is a natural aftereffect. That is perhaps the reason for this bizarre feeling.'*

I switched off the lights and went to bed. Through the large open window by my bedside, I could see the backyard garden. The soothing white hue of the moonlight was washing the trees and the shrubs with its soft elegance. I had deliberately kept the window open so that some cool and fresh air could float inside the room. As I watched the scenic natural beauty, I fell asleep.

I don't know for how long I slept, but it wasn't more than an hour when my sleep was disrupted suddenly. I was shocked by an unexpected uncanny feeling. The eerie consciousness made me feel as if somebody was standing near the open window. It seemed I would be able to see that apparition if I simply lifted my head. That realization crumpled my courage, and a massive shroud of fear clutched my entire body. Once again, I was unable to understand the reason behind that terror. I didn't dare to look outside, but I could visualize that some apparition was holding the iron rails of the window and staring at me with his red glaring eyes!

With all my might, I closed my eyes tightly. I was determined that I won't look out the window. I was too petrified to confront the ghost. I tried to calm my mind and go to sleep, but I failed miserably.

Subsequently, a horrible smell filled the room. I wondered . . . *'Has a rat died somewhere inside the house? No . . . that isn't possible. I would have smelled it immediately after coming back.'*

It seemed that the eerie smell was the result of a horrible concoction of iodine, lint, cream, and the stench from a festering wound. I felt angry with the caretaker, and cursed him, "These people are useless! They don't even care to keep the house clean. This place was uninhabited for almost the entire year. And even then they don't bother to keep it clean."

An uncanny voice echoed inside my mind . . .

Suren . . . Oh, Suren . . . Look at the window. Just once, please! Turn your head and look at it . . .

A peculiar creepiness gripped the entire house. It was like an evil omen that was fierce, wild, and restless. I cannot express that feeling in words. I could sense that I was in great danger. It was a peril that could take me up to the doorsteps of death. I would just have to step a foot ahead to enter the frozen and icy darkness of the otherworld that we all know as Hell.

"No, I will not do that . . . I will not look at the window. I will not open my eyes and stare at the devilish sight," I struggled to convince my mind.

A paranormal influence was hypnotizing everything around me. Yet, it was outside the walls of the house. It didn't have the power to percolate vaporously inside the house. For ages, my forefathers had worshipped the divine deities of *Vastu* inside that house. The strength of the devout blessings of those Gods prevented the omen to enter. It was powerless within the four walls of the house. My subconscious mind consoled me with this reasoning. It is true that inside a thick blanket of darkness and seclusion, the subconscious becomes audible to the heart.

Something moved outside the window and the sound startled me. It was a creepy sound. It seemed that somebody was tapping on the iron rails of the window and trying to attract my attention. Once . . . twice . . . thrice . . . My heart started to beat faster and faster.

'Should I look and see?' I asked myself again.

Then, suddenly, I remembered that a weasel had made its den inside the timber beams on the roof. I saw it in the evening too.

With a startle, I said to myself, *'Yes! It's the weasel that is making the noise. It must have caught some insects and is feasting on them.'*

Like magic, my courage returned the moment I had the realization. It felt like a throbbing fever had vanished miraculously, leaving me with a sense of soothing release. I turned away to sleep and said to myself, *'Ah . . . it is so true. When the body is tired, the mind plays such games!'*

I sighed of relief and tried to sleep. But the moments didn't last long. The strange feeling kept returning to my mind . . .

'Tonight, I am not alone. Someone else is present too. That ghost is keeping a savage vigil on me with its sleepless eyes. It won't let me rest tonight. Not even for a moment.'

Each time I was about to fall asleep, an uncanny panic dragged me back to consciousness. I felt scared to open my eyes or sit up on the bed. That eerie tapping sound persisted on the window rails. Then, a faint thumping noise on the door joined that cacophony.

The sounds echoed in my house . . .

Suren . . . Open your eyes. Suren . . . turn back and look at the window . . .

My body started to sweat profusely and wet the entire bed. Yet, I remained glued to the it and prayed for the dawn to arrive. Finally, as the morning broke, and the sounds of human voices floated through the window, my fear gently precipitated. Soon, my tired body fell asleep, and I slept till nine o' clock in the morning.

When I woke up, not even a single drop of fear remained. I had some tea and went out to stroll around the neighborhood.

While I was roaming around, again, a strange incident happened. At that time, I didn't pay much attention to that episode. Yet, shivers ran down my spine when I thought of it later. On my way, I met the neighborhood uncle, whom I intended to meet and wanted to show the medal. The previous night, I had planned to meet him, so I had carried the medal with me, but it had skipped my mind while I was attending Vrindavan's dinner invitation.

He saw me and said, "Hello Suren, I hope you are doing good. Last night, I noticed you in the neighborhood. It was quite late at that time, so I didn't call you. I guess you were returning from Vrindavan's house, right? I was strolling on the rooftop. To be honest, I didn't call you because I noticed a gentleman walking along with you. Who is he? He seems like a stranger to me. He was very tall, just like someone from Punjab. Looking at his stature, it seemed that he was probably not a Bengali. Is he your friend?"

I was left in complete awe, and I kept looking at his face. His words had made me speechless. I exclaimed, "Last night you saw a tall gentleman walking with me? Uncle, what are you saying?"

The old man was equally surprised and replied, "Are you saying that there wasn't anyone with you last night? Do you mean, you were walking alone? Suren, I might be old but my eyesight isn't that bad."

I laughed and tried to put him at ease. I said, "No uncle, I really don't intend to mean so. Perhaps, due to the darkness, you might have been mistaken. Doesn't it sometimes happen to all of us?"

The old man was more puzzled at my answer. He responded, "But . . . that is so peculiar! How could my vision deceive me so much? I saw it clearly. You came around the mango tree and switched on the battery-powered torchlight. In that light, I undoubtedly saw a tall gentleman who was walking behind you. Then, you switched off the torchlight and walked into the shadow under the mango tree. The moonlight had kept the entire place illuminated and everything was quite clearly visible. In that soft white light, I saw the tall man closely following you. Even though it was dark, I could see his silhouette. At one point, I even thought I should call and ask you who he was. But I chose not to because it was late in the night . . . Was it all a mistake of fainting eyesight? Do you really think so?"

Once more, I tried to convince him that nobody was with me and that I was completely alone. I tried to persuade him that it was a mistake of his own eyesight. However, I don't think my reasoning totally convinced him.

I spent the rest of the day in Vrindavan's company, and we chit-chatted for hours. In clear daylight, the previous night's ghostly experience felt comical. I was ashamed of my own naivety, so I didn't reveal anything to Vrindavan. That day, I had planned to board the night train to return to Kolkata. After having some tea with Vrindavan in the evening, I bid him farewell and went back to my ancestral home to finish my packing. Then, I took my suitcase and headed out toward the railway station. The time was well past the sunset, and the dark evening's veil had covered the entire landscape around the village.

I was walking through the enormous grove in Bauripara. It was so big that one usually took five to six minutes to cross it with long strides. I was almost in the middle of the grove when I heard something from behind. I stopped abruptly and looked back. But a sudden gust of fear shook me to the core.

At a distance, near the corner of the thicket, I clearly saw the outline of a human figure, an abominable male figure! In the dim combination of light and darkness, it was the outline of a strange being. The man was monstrously tall and wore a weird, elongated horsehair cap that was strapped by a thin metallic chain that went past his chin. I had seen such caps in old portraits of English soldiers. The figure stood there motionless, staring at me with a frozen frown.

The figure was about ten yards away from me, or perhaps, even less. In that situation of desperate helplessness, I gathered my courage and walked up a few paces toward the figure. I needed to find the meaning of all that was happening to me. I felt desperate to seek the truth. I felt a strange urge to quench the thirst of my curiosity. However, the situation was becoming stranger with every passing moment. Even after I walked up a few paces, the figure remained absolutely motionless, as if it were a statue that was carved out of stone! I was then about seven or eight yards away from the figure. Even the metallic strap of his horsehair cap was clearly visible to me. But the figure stood there with a stone-cold stillness.

I realized that my feet were trembling with fear, and I was unable to hold onto my own balance. My head started to feel light, as though I was about to faint. I lost every bit of my strength to move myself away from the spot where I was standing. I was almost glued to the ground as I stood there and faced my monstrous nemesis.

To be honest, I wouldn't have survived if I had stood there for another thirty seconds or more. But something miraculous happened and I am still thankful that it did. Across the trail through the enormous grove in Bauripara, I heard human footsteps. I looked around and noticed that four or five men were moving around in the woods. They were holding burning torches and traversing along the trailing path. I gathered all my strength and screamed. To attract their attention, I screamed as loud as I could. The men heard me and came running.

The men hurried up to me and were stunned to see me. One of them asked, "Babu, what happened?"

Another one held his burning torch near my face and said, "Oh Babu, what is there? What happened to you? Your face has turned completely pale. Did something petrify you? This Bauripara grove is not a very safe place. Many people fear coming here after dark. Has something terrified you too?"

In the light of their torches, I noticed with alarm that the apparition of a monstrously tall figure was still standing there.

One of the men asked me, "What are you looking at? Babu, are you looking at that weird demon tree beside that mango tree?"

Another commented, "It seems that the demon tree's branches have been cut and the trash is piled up under it. In the darkness, it can easily be mistaken as a gigantic human figure standing in the woods . . . Babu, come with us. Let us go from here."

As we were leaving, I looked back once again. This time, I didn't see any abominable figure. It was indeed the demon tree that was surrounded by its cut-down foliage. I laughed at my own stupidity and said to myself, "Oh, it was such a huge mistake. I was unnecessarily deceived by the sight. Ah . . . and I was telling my old uncle that his eyesight has become weak!"

The men helped me reach the railway station. I thanked them and boarded the train. The next morning, I returned the medal to Sudhir.

He took it back and said, "Sir, my grandfather wants to meet you. He has requested you to come and visit him after school. I will take you along."

I felt inquisitive, so I agreed.

That evening, Sudhir's grandfather told me another strange tale. He sat in front of me and said, "Suren Babu, I am so glad that you have come back safely. I was extremely worried about you when I heard that you had taken the medal from Sudhir. I didn't know the address of your ancestral home, or else, I would have sent you a telegram. That medal was given to my father by an English soldier. The incident happened much before I was born. He had mortgaged it to my father but couldn't take it back. He forfeited it. But that man was very suborned and was a drunkard."

Sudhir's grandfather looked at me and continued, "Suren Babu, there is an inherent danger that looms over that cursed medal. It is ghostly. If anybody outside our family's bloodline possesses it, that medal brings grave peril to that person. It is like a paranormal curse that tries to harm any person who takes it. Many years ago, a terrible incident occurred. A close relative of ours, one of my sister's husbands, was so overwhelmed by the splendor of the medal that he pleaded and then took it home for a few days. He wanted to show it to his family. Unfortunately, great misfortune struck that very night. In the late hours of the fateful evening, he mysteriously fell from the roof and died. And, in the pocket of the corpse, we found the cursed medal."

I sat like an immovable puppet and said in a mechanical dry voice, "Fell from the roof? The medal was found in his pocket?"

"Yes, Suren Babu," replied Sudhir's grandfather in a grim voice, "he was my brother-in-law and somebody whom I adored. I won't lie about him. That unfortunate incident happened twenty seven years ago, but it is still fresh in my memory. A few more people had taken it later, but they all returned it within a day. Each one of them had complained of strange ghostly occurrences and experiences during the night while the medal was in their possession. Each one of them felt that somebody was following them like a shadow that would plunge upon them with its monstrous ghastliness."

Sudhir's grandfather held my hand and said, "That cursed medal is not suited for everyone. It has an evil power to summon death upon the possessor if that person doesn't belong to our bloodline. That is the reason why I was worried about your safety and was desperately looking for your address to send you a telegram. However, now I feel relieved."

That evening, I couldn't say anything. I just went back home.

*

A month after that day, I went back to my ancestral home again. Once more, I went inside the Bauripara grove and visited the location where I had seen that monstrous apparition. It was daytime and the entire place was fully illuminated by the sunlight. Strangely, I couldn't find that demon tree anywhere. It had mysteriously evaporated. I searched thoroughly. I found the mango tree, beside which the demon tree was supposed to be. However, it was not there. Surprisingly, there was no sign of it. I looked at the ground to see if somebody had cut the tree down. But I didn't find anything! The place was clean, as if no demon tree ever existed at that spot.

Why did the apparition visit Suren? Why did Suren have suicidal thoughts? Why was he saved mysteriously? Did the paranormal medal still attract its owner?

Nobody knew the correct answers.

***

In the Forest of Bomaiburu

It was a time when at the behest of the government, the jungles were being surveyed. Six miles away from our Head Office of the Forest Department, inside the Bomaiburu Jungle, Ramchandra Singh was posted as a surveyor of that region. He was an able and long-serving employee of our Forest Department. One morning, word came that Ramchandra Singh had gone mad! It was said that Ramchandra's mind had been totally deranged, leading him to complete lunacy. It was a shocking news, as there was no reason why a perfectly healthy man would suddenly become a lunatic. Without wasting any time, I took a few others with me and rushed to check on the matter.

Bomaiburu Jungle was not very dense but was completely uninhabited by humans. It comprised sparse woodlands across vast rugged terrains that were occasionally scattered with large trees. The aerial roots of those tall trees came down from the branches and looked like the downhauls of some enormous ships.

At a distance from the woods, in the open grassland, we saw two small huts. As we reached, we deciphered that the relatively larger one belonged to Ramchandra Singh while the smaller one belonged to his attendant, Ashrafi Tindal.

We saw that Ramchandra Singh was lying down on his cot with his eyes closed. When he saw us, he got up hurriedly.

I asked, "Ramchandra, what happened to you? How are you feeling now?"

With his head bowed down, Ramchandra clasped his hands and stood in silence.

However, Ashrafi came forward and revealed a strange tale of their inexplicable ordeal . . . "Hazoor, something strange and inexplicable has happened. If you'll hear about it, you won't be able to believe it. I would've personally come to the Head Office to deliver the news, but I was afraid to leave Surveyor Sahib alone in this jungle. It all started a few days ago when Surveyor Sahib began to complain about a dog that came and disturbed him during the night. Babu, I live in that adjacent small hut and Surveyor Sahib lives here in this place.

"Each day he complained, 'I don't understand from where a white dog comes every night. My bed is atop the bamboo platform in this room and every night that mysterious dog sneaks under it. In the darkness, it whines and, at times, even tries to snuggle with me from behind. I try to ignore it, but that animal keeps coming back every night.'

"Then, four days ago, it was very late in the night when Surveyor Sahib called me hastily and said, 'Ashrafi, come quickly. That dog has come again! I caught it by its tail. Quick, bring along a stick.'

"I woke up hurriedly, took a stick and a lantern, and rushed out. But, as I reached his hut, I was frozen with disbelief, and I am sure that you too wouldn't believe what I am going to tell. Hazoor, I cannot dare to tell lies in front of you. Please trust my words . . .

"That night, as I was about to enter his hut, I saw a young woman rush out from inside! She ran out and then disappeared into the jungle. The awkwardness of the incident left me puzzled for a few moments. However, I gathered my senses and went inside quickly. In the darkness, Surveyor Sahib was groping for a matchbox on the floor.

"He saw me and said, 'Ashrafi, did you see that dog?'

"I replied, 'Where is the dog? Sahib, I just saw a young woman rush out from here!'

"He replied angrily, 'You scoundrel, are you trying to stalk me? You shall pay for this impertinence! Why will a young woman come inside my hut in this barren jungle? I had caught that dog by its tail. There is no doubt about it. Its long ears even touched my body. It was hiding under my bed and was moaning constantly. How can you say that it was a woman who was inside my hut? Ashrafi, have you started to indulge yourself in the vices of addiction? Beware of my heed, or else I will lodge a complaint against you at the head office!'

"Hazoor, the following night, till very late, I stayed alert to keep a strict vigil. However, the moment I felt a bit drowsy, I heard Surveyor Sahib's voice. He was calling me aloud. Without wasting time, I ran out of my hut and reached his doorstep when, once again, I saw her! Yes, a young woman came out of his hut and crossed the bamboo fencing on the northern boundary. She jumped across it and then entered the jungle. Almost immediately, I ran after her and entered the jungle too. It was impossible for anybody to hide anywhere in the jungle. I was confident that she wouldn't be able to escape. Hazoor, I have worked in jungle surveys for years and I am familiar with every nook and corner of these woods. But that night, I was left dumbfounded. I thoroughly combed the entire area but failed to find even a trace of that woman.

"Then, I felt suspicious. I took my lantern and scrutinized the ground. What I saw was even more uncanny! Other than the marks of my own shoes, there were no other footprints on the soil. Hazoor, it was ghostly! It was impossible.

"That night, I didn't tell anything to Surveyor Sahib. We were two sole human beings inside this huge, mysterious, and dark jungle. Chills of fear ran down my spine and the ghostly event numbed me. I remembered an evil repute that is still associated with Bomaiburu Jungle. When I was young, my grandfather told me that this jungle was infamous for being uncannily notorious. Once, he told me something very bizarre. Hazoor, do you see that big Banyan tree atop that adjacent hill? Many years ago, my grandfather was returning from Purniya after work. It was quite late in the night, and he was riding his horse, carrying a good amount of cash with him. As he reached close to the Banyan tree, he was stunned by the sight of a group of extremely beautiful, young women who were dancing and playing under the tree in the moonlight. Hazoor, in the local folklore, those creatures are called *Damabanu*. They are paranormal beings who can be classified as D*jinn Pari*, and who live in these barren jungles! They are ghastly creatures who can even murder unsuspecting and helpless human beings! My grandfather was lucky enough to escape that night.

"Hazoor, coming back to the present situation . . . the next night, I decided to stay with Surveyor Sahib, inside his hut. Throughout the entire night, I stayed awake and remained alert. To remain awake, I busied myself with the calculations of our survey work and scrutinized our progress.

It was perhaps very late in the night, and I felt a bit sleepy when I was jolted back to my senses by a sudden noise. I lifted my head and looked up. Surveyor Sahib was fast asleep, but I clearly saw something quickly crawl under his bed.

"Startled, I leapt on my feet and peered under the bed. The dim light within the hut cast an eerie glow and as I lowered my head, I was shocked! At first, I thought that a young woman was crouched under that bed. And she was looking at me with an uncanny hypnotic smile. Yes, Hazoor . . . Yes, I swear that I saw her without any mistake! I could even see her long dark hair elegantly gathered into a thick bundle.

"My lantern was on the table where I was sitting and working inside that room. It was only a few feet away. To take a closer look, I got up to fetch the lantern, when something dashed out from under the bed, brushed past me and ran into the open. The table, where I had kept the lantern, was adjacent to the door. In the moderate glow of that lantern, I clearly saw that it was a huge white dog! Please believe me, Hazoor, the animal was totally white in color with not even a single black spot on its entire body.

"In that commotion, Surveyor Sahib woke up and asked, 'What? What was it?'

"I steadied my nerves and replied calmly, 'Oh, it's nothing. I guess a fox, or a wild dog might have sneaked in.'

"'Dog?' he exclaimed, 'What kind of dog?'

"'Sahib, it was a white dog,' I replied.

"'White dog!' he sighed helplessly and said, 'Was it a white dog? Did you see it properly? Was it white or was it a black one?'

"I answered, 'Sahib, it was indeed a white dog.'

"I was surprised because I couldn't comprehend how the color of the dog mattered so much. I didn't know what the difference would've been if it were a black dog. In that helpless state, Surveyor Sahib slowly reclined himself onto the bed and fell asleep mechanically.

"A blanket of uneasiness grasped me from all sides, and I started to feel scared. I was too scared to even close my eyes for once! Drowned in that ocean of terror, I sat there throughout the night. When the faint rays of the new dawn started to come in, I once again looked under the bed. I wanted to examine the place once more, but I was appalled to find a bunch of long black hair under the bed. Yes,

I found them, and I have kept them to myself. They definitely belong to a woman, but how did they go under the bed? The feminine locks were soft and black. No Hazoor, furry dogs, especially white ones, don't have such black and long hair. It belonged to some uncanny feminine presence inside this room that night.

"It has been three days since that fateful dawn. Over these three days, Surveyor Sahib has lost his sanity. Hazoor, I am petrified. Is it now my turn to go mad? Please save me . . ."

The queer narration of Ashrafi Tindal's uncanny experience seemed like a fable. Even after taking that bunch of black hair in my own hands, I wasn't convinced enough to believe everything that he told us. There was no doubt that it was a bunch of black feminine hair, but that didn't prove anything. Moreover, Ashrafi was an old man, and it was quite possible that he was himself a slave of intoxicating vices. Under the influence of such things, people often tend to hallucinate. Inside that vast Bomaiburu Jungle, the nearest human colony was Labhtuliya, which was six miles away from their makeshift huts. Then, how was it possible for a young woman to visit them during the night? Moreover, the local villagers were fully aware of the dangers of wild animals like tigers and wild boars, and they seldom ventured out during night-time.

If I were to believe Ashrafi Tindal, then whatever he had confessed was highly mysterious and eerie. If I were to believe him then I needed to trust that the forsaken Bomaiburu Jungle, and its vast uninhabited pastures, were shadowy lands where horrific supernatural occurrences of the medieval era were still strongly prevalent. The civilized worlds of neither the twentieth century nor the nineteenth century had yet found their way into it. So, the uncanny paranormal happenings were still a harsh reality in those frontiers.

Considering the situation, I ordered an immediate evacuation of the site. We suspended all the survey work in that location, wrapped up the tents, took Ramchandra Singh and Ashrafi Tindal with us, and went back. However, Ramchandra Singh didn't recover from his illness. His lunacy overwhelmed him completely. In his madness, he used to scream, laugh, and sing aloud throughout the night. We kept him under our supervision inside the head office of our forest department and we even sought the help of numerous doctors. Sadly, nothing worked, and the poor man couldn't recover. At last, a distant cousin of his took him back to their ancestral village.

*

Six months later, it was around the month of *Chaitra*[12], when two people came to meet me at the head office. One of them was an aged man, a cattle grazer who was about sixty-five years old, and the other was a young man of about twenty or twenty-two years. The father-son duo belonged to a distant village in the districts and had come to request to lease some grassland from the Forest Department. Against their payment of revenue, they requested that I lease a piece of land where they could graze their cattle.

At the time, most of the grasslands in our jurisdiction had already been rented. Only a small portion of it, inside the Bomaiburu Jungle, was available. Their request was genuine, and I gave them my consent. Then, I made the necessary arrangements to lease that land to them. As the job was done smoothly, the father-son duo went away happily.

A few days later, they came to visit me once again. The two of them looked happy and content. The old man said joyfully, "Hazoor, the jungle is lovely. The piece of land that you have given us has such beautiful long grass. This would not have been possible

---

[12] Chaitra is the last month in the Bengali calendar. It falls from mid-March to mid-April and is the last month of Spring.

if you hadn't helped us. We would never have got a grassland like this for our cattle."

I had almost forgotten about Ramchandra Singh and Ashrafi Tindal's episode. But, even if I did remember, I don't think I would've wanted to tell about their fateful experience to the happy father and son. I had no intention to scare them unnecessarily. Moreover, scaring them away would mean a potential loss to the State because none of the residents were willing to rent a piece of land inside the Bomaiburu Jungle, especially after the incident with Ramchandra Singh. They considered it cursed.

After a few days, it was the month of Baisakh. One day, the old man came to my office again. He seemed angry while his son followed him with an anxious face.

I asked, "What happened?"

The old man exclaimed angrily, "Hazoor, I feel ashamed to tell this to you, but I must do it. This worthless son of mine has taken up a filthy habit. I feel embarrassed to even speak of his lewd deeds. For the last seven or eight days, I have noticed a young woman leaving our hut. Hazoor, we live in a small, thatched shack inside the jungle with enough space to house just the two of us. Inside that little space, it is not easy to deceive my eyes. After I noticed that heinous incident for two consecutive days, I confronted my son, but he was totally taken aback! He said. 'No, I promise that I don't know anything.' So, I didn't do anything further. Then, once again, for the next two days, I observed the same thing. I saw a young woman stealthily escaping from our hut in the middle of the night!"

The old man was agitated with rage and howled, "Hazoor, I felt like beating up my own son. How can a father let his son indulge in such a sin? I just cannot see him become impious in front of my own eyes! Unfortunately, the immoral wickedness of this boy didn't come to an end. Last night, I witnessed the same incident again. Hence, I have dragged him here along with me today. Hazoor, now everything is in your hands. Please do justice to us. Please caution him against such filthy and sinful acts of lewdness."

The old man's heartfelt appeal suddenly brought back bitter memories of the fateful incident that happened a few months ago with Ramchandra Singh. The memories came like a gust of harsh wind, and I felt a pinch in my heart.

I asked, "At what hour of the night did you observe it?"

The old man replied, "Each time, it was almost during the last couple of hours before dawn."

"Are you sure? Was it really a young woman?" I asked again.

"Hazoor, my eyesight is not so weak," said the old man. "Yes, I can vouch that each time it was a young woman. One night, she was wearing a clear white saree. On another, she wore a red one. Another day, she wore a black one. One night, when she was quietly escaping, I followed her stealthily. Unfortunately, she vanished behind the thicket of Kans grass and I lost her trail. I hurried back to the hut and saw my son fast asleep. I knew he was feigning, so I pushed him, and he sat up in wonder. Hazoor, I know he was trying to deceive me. He is a liar and has become a slave to lust. Hazoor, I urge you with all my heart. The medicine for this shameful disease is only in your hands! Only your strict words can strike fear in his heart and bring him back to his senses. Nothing else can cure him. Hazoor, please help us."

I took the boy aside to a corner, and asked him strictly, "What is all this nonsense that I am hearing about you? What are you up to? Tell me everything."

The boy held my feet and wept, "Hazoor, no! I am not doing anything that is impious! I don't have any idea what my Baba is saying. Throughout the day I roam around in the forest and graze the cattle. After the entire day's hard work, I sleep like a dead horse at night. That sleep is so deep that even if the house is on fire, I won't wake up!"

I questioned him sternly, "Tell me honestly, haven't you ever seen anything enter your house at night?"

He pleaded, "Please believe me, I have not seen anything. My sleep is too deep, and I don't know anything that my father is confessing. I haven't done anything wrong!"

I didn't probe him further. Something was bothering my subconscious mind and I chose not to make things difficult for the boy. The old man felt content that I had scolded his son and had warned him of any misdoings. Hence, the father-son duo went back happily. A fortnight passed and then, one day, the boy came to visit me alone.

He said, "Hazoor, I wanted to ask you something. That day, when my Baba brought me to you, why did you ask that question? Hazoor, why did you ask me if I had seen anything enter our house at night?"

"Why? What is the matter?" I asked with suspicion.

"Hazoor, recently my sleep has become lighter," he replied, "it is not so deep anymore. An apprehension brews within my heart every night due to some unknown reason. Or maybe it is an elusive anxiety that plays within my mind because Baba is always skeptical about my nightly whereabouts and is himself worried. But Hazoor, for the past few nights, I have noticed a white dog enter our house during the late hours of the night. It comes very late when the night is deep. Many times, when my sleep disrupted, I have seen it loitering near the bed too. Each time, as soon as I woke up, it ran away. I don't know how it understands that I am awake. The same thing repeated for a few nights."

Without a word, I listened to his peculiar tale. He continued, "Hazoor, last night something strange happened, but Baba is unaware of it. I have come here secretly to tell you everything. When I woke up last night, the white dog had already sneaked inside our hut. As my sleep was interrupted, I saw it was leaving quietly. With uncontrolled curiosity, I tried to observe what it was doing. Through the open window, I saw that the dog went out toward the white thicket of Kans grass. Then, within the blink of my eyes, I saw that it was no longer a dog! It was a beautiful young woman, who was slowly walking out into the woods. Hazoor, with sheer disbelief, I ran out, but as I stood in the open, there was nobody. That woman had magically vanished into thin air. I was horrified by that uncanny episode. I didn't say anything to Baba. Throughout the entire time, he was fast asleep. He is an old man, and it is useless to plant the seeds of fear in his frail heart. Hazoor, I don't know what happened and what I had seen. What is it Hazoor? Please tell me."

His words unnerved me too, but I gathered my wits, tried to calm him down and erase his fears. I told him, "Oh, it is nothing. Your sleep-ridden eyes must have deceived you. However, if you and your Baba feel scared to sleep in the forest during the night, I would be happy to make accommodations so that you two can come here every night and sleep inside the Forest Office's premises."

Perhaps, the young boy felt ashamed of his lack of courage and went away without any more discussion. However, the uneasiness within my own heart refused to leave me. Hence, I made up my mind that if one more complaint came from either of the two of them, I would make the necessary arrangements to allocate two night guards to their hut inside the Bomaiburu Jungle. Sadly, I failed to gauge the severity of the danger that was looming; the ruthless assault of the unknown came down like an unexpected and sudden bolt of thunder.

Three days later . . .

I had just woken up in the morning when I got to know that the old cattle grazer's son had died. The shock of that news unnerved me to the core, and I rushed out on my horseback, and headed toward their hut inside the Bomaiburu Jungle.

As I reached, I saw that the young boy's corpse was still there. The lifeless body of the innocent young boy was lying in the wild bushes of the Kans grass woods. His face, now devoid of life, reflected a clear expression of sheer horror, as if he had confronted some ghastly apparition which caused an enormous blow of terror and had plucked away his life from his body.

The old man was completely shattered with grief. He revealed, "Hazoor, a few hours before dawn, my sleep was disrupted and I woke up. I saw that my son was not on his bed. Immediately, I took a lantern and rushed out to search for him in the forest. Unfortunately, even as I combed the surrounding woods, I failed to find him in the dark. Then, as the dawn broke, I saw the lifeless body of my unfortunate child lying here . . ."

It seemed to me that the boy was woken up by a sudden occurrence and driven by curiosity, he might have chased it and hurried out into the forest. We discovered a broken lantern and a thick stick near the lad's corpse, and it strengthened my conviction about what might have happened on that fateful night.

'What was he chasing? What drove him to such madness that he picked up the stick and the lantern and rushed out into the forest? Why weren't there any footmarks on the soft wet soil, other than those of the boy's? How was that possible? What was he chasing?'

Perhaps these questions were destined to remain unanswered forever.

There were no wounds on the corpse. Death seemed to have come down as a dark curtain of fear and had stopped the boy's heart without even touching him.

The mystery behind the unusual death of that young boy remained unsolved.

The police couldn't find any clue about the case and went back without any success. Such was the shock of that incident that the local villagers thereafter didn't dare to traverse close to the Bomaiburu Jungle, even hours before the sun went down.

The aftershock of that horrific episode didn't spare me either. For many nights, I remained awake for hours in the night on my bed as my skeptical and fearful eyes scanned the vast open landscape around my living quarters at the head office of the forest department. Every night, the vast wilderness, soaked in the melancholy silvery hue of the moonlight, confronted my heart with its colossal and pale countenance, like a gigantic apparition that was secretly trying to consume me. The soundless barrenness of the Bomaiburu Jungle created ripples of terror within my heart, as I remained sleepless within the shroud of an unknown and unseen fear during the nights.

My heart used to whisper to me, *'This place is unholy. Run . . . Run away to Kolkata. This place is not fit for human beings. The moonlit barren landscape of these woodlands is the kingdom of the nocturnal devils of ancient folklore. The devilish witches mentioned in those tales are creatures of the undead in these lands. Those ghastly beings would deceive you and lead you to your horrible demise. Run . . . run away, and never return.'*

Some questions are beyond the borders of explanation . . .

What were the apparitions of the Bomaiburu Forest? Whom did those ghastly creatures choose as their victims? Why did they oppose human intervention?

***

The Shadowy Portrait

This is a story that I have heard from a friend, and I trust every word of his to be true. He is a man who has traveled across the world and is well-educated and kind-hearted. He has a jolly personality, which makes him a fun-loving guy. On many occasions, I have spent nights listening to the tales of his vivid experiences in his own wonderful narration.

In the course of our lives, we cross paths with countless individuals with diverse personalities. Many of these people become part of our daily routines in the workplace too. However, despite spending hours with such people, and even after addressing them with reverence, a certain emotional distance remains, making it rare to find companionship with whom we can share our deepest thoughts and spend hours in heartfelt conversation.

My friend Samar, however, was somebody who is totally different. I always feel a craving to be in his company and listen to his stories. He is one of those people who makes one feel happy.

*

It was a damp monsoon afternoon, and I was sitting idly inside my house in the suburbs. The monotony of the continuous downpours created a melancholy in my heart, and I was bored. Unable to cope with the boredom, I headed out of my house, boarded a train, and reached Kolkata. The city's tramlines were closed due to the heavy rain, and the streets were devoid of buses. Therefore, without any hope of a local commute, I decided to walk down to Samar's house.

Samar was overjoyed by my sudden and unexpected visit. He took me inside and made some hot tea and warm refreshments. We sat inside his living room and relished the food. Then, I stretched myself on the cozy and well-cushioned armchair while Samar sat beside me.

As the evening closed in, it started to rain profusely.

Samar was always a great host for all his guests. For me, as one of his closest friends, it was bound to be even more special. He said, "Come, let's go upstairs. You don't need to go back home tonight. My humble kitchen has a decently functional stove and enough supplies for both of us. I will ask Raghu to make *Khichuri*[13] for dinner. Eggs and potatoes are there in the pantry and they would be the perfect accompaniments for a hot meal of Khichuri. Should I send Raghu to fetch some fish from the bazaar?"

"No, Samar. The arrangements are perfect," I replied, "Khichuri with fried eggs and boiled potatoes sounds like an excellent dinner to enjoy the monsoons!"

"Fantastic. So, let us go upstairs. I am not letting you leave in this bad weather. You shall stay here tonight, and we can chat for hours."

---

[13] Khichuri is a delicious one-pot meal of rice, moong lentils and mixed vegetables. It is a perfect comfort food for the Bengalis.

The library on the first floor of Samar's house was a delectable place for any book lover. With hundreds of books crowding over the bookshelves, it was a room that was like a reservoir of knowledge. Most of those books were either about science or history. The adjacent walls were adorned with oil paintings of Himalayan landscapes by distinguished painters. Samar was extremely fond of the Himalayas. Its beauty had always mesmerized him. He was utterly proficient in every geographical intricacy of the region. I had spent many nights listening to the fascinating tales of his Himalayan rendezvous.

To explain briefly, the library room carried a classy vibe of taste and knowledge.

Upon the writing desk, there was an open book of photographs. Samar picked it up and said, "Have you seen this? This is a Himalayan Journal. It is a travelogue by Sven Hedin."

"Really?" I asked, "of which place?"

"Kashmir," Samar replied excitedly.

"I didn't know that Sven Hedin had also traveled to such luxurious locations," I laughed. "I thought he used to visit remote places like Taklamakan or Karakorum."

"No, he did visit Kashmir and see what a fantastic description he has provided in this travelogue! He really had an eye for nature's unending beauty," added Samar.

Hence, our conversation gradually changed to the subject of Kashmir. It was a place that was like a pilgrimage for Samar. Many times, he had visited Kashmir to rejuvenate his tired heart and mind after months of monotonous hard work in the fast-paced city of Kolkata. He was an avid traveler who always sought refuge in the oasis of Mother Nature's lap whenever he felt worn out.

Every time he visited Kashmir, Samar heartily praised the subtle beauty of the place. However, that night, he said something different . . . very different.

That day, Samar told me about a supernatural occurrence. He revealed how he had a paranormal experience while he was once traveling to Kashmir.

Let me pen down his story precisely as he narrated it . . .

*

That year, after the Durga Puja festivities, my friend Rathikant Maitra and I decided to go on a road trip on his motorcar to Kashmir. Rathikant had a habit to go on one such trip every year where he sets out on his car and drives for miles along the Grand Trunk Road to various destinations. So, the two of us decided to go together that year. As we enjoyed the pangs and pleasures of the long drive, we finally reached Delhi. We stayed there for two days to take some rest and rejuvenate ourselves, and then resumed the trip. With us were Ramdeen, our cleaner, and Nathu, our servant. The rest of the journey was unhindered and lively, and I shall refrain from describing those moments.

Three days later, we reached Kohala. It was almost evening, and we stopped the vehicle at the local bazaar to have some tea and refreshments. Ramdeen and Nathu finished their tea quickly and went back to the car, while Rathikant and I sat on a wooden bench beside the teashop.

As we sipped our tea, we asked the owner of the teashop for a decent place where we could spend the night. The man gave us a few options, so we took Ramdeen with us and went out in search of a shelter to spend the night. All of us were tired and we needed a good night's sleep to get refreshed before the next day's journey. Nathu was made to stay back with the car.

As we went, Rathikant asked, "We need to find a shelter for the car too."

"Yes, we better find one for it," I replied, "or else, Nathu would freeze inside the vehicle in this bitter cold."

"I believe Ramdeen can endure any such extremities," I added with a smirk.

"Yes, Babu!" replied Ramdeen with an energized voice, "Don't worry about me. I can withstand everything."

Unfortunately, our search for a shelter was fruitless, and we failed to find any place where we could spend the night. Kohala is a small village. The few dingy motels at the local bazaar were already overcrowded with truck drivers from Punjab. It was impossible to squeeze in amid those crammed places. One local shop owner gave us hope and said that there was a small room behind his shop. However, the room was unclean and had no ventilation; it would have been impossible to spend even a few hours inside it. Moreover, there was no option to park the car under a shelter. Even though we were joking about Ramdeen's herculean strength, it was humanly impossible for us to make him sleep inside the car on that freezing night.

As we lost all hope, Rathikant asked, "What to do now?"

"I am absolutely clueless," I replied sadly.

Hence, as a last resort, we decided to return to the teashop and ask the owner to help us somehow. We pleaded him desperately, as if he was our only messiah upon whom we have vested all our hopes when we had embarked upon our two-thousand miles long journey.

The owner of the teashop was a good man. He listened to our earnest plea and said, "Babu, there is one last option. Behind this bazaar, that little alley goes across that small hill. Beyond that hill lives an old Jat man. I have heard that at times, he has given shelter to travelers to spend a night in his house."

It was our last ray of hope and we headed out to seek that old Jat man's house. Rathikant and I reached the place and saw a two-storey wooden house whose residual glamor reflected the fact that its owner was once a well-to-do person.

We knocked on the door and called out aloud. Soon, the door was opened and an old man with a long white beard and a decently strong physique came out.

He looked at us and said in a harsh voice, "Why are you creating a ruckus? Who are you?"

With utmost politeness, we described our helpless situation and expressed our plea for his help as our last resort. I added, "We are harmless travelers, and we don't have any intention of creating any chaos. Please help us."

"Where are you coming from?" asked the old man.

"Kolkata," Rathikant replied.

"Who told you to come to my house for shelter?" inquired the old man.

"We heard it at the bazaar," I responded.

"No," said the old man, "I don't rent rooms in my house anymore."

"We request you," I requested, "please help us just for tonight. We are helpless and have come to seek your help because . . ."

The old man interrupted and paused for a while. Then, he asked, "How many of you are there?"

"There are only four of us," added Rathikant.

"Well, I won't be able to provide more than a single room." replied the old man sternly.

"We would be absolutely grateful to you if you could give us that one room to spend the night," I replied earnestly.

Without any more words, the man turned back and asked us to follow him while he started to climb up the stairs that led to the first floor of his house. His behavior was peculiar and a sense of eeriness mingled with the entire atmosphere. However, even in that hazy mysteriousness of the surroundings, we followed him quietly.

It seemed that his house was devoid of any feminine presence and he lived there all alone.

As we reached upstairs, the man took us to a room on the left corner beside the staircase and said grimly, "I can give you this room. There are no other rooms available in this house. Spread the carpet on the floor. The earthen pot outside, beside the staircase, has water. Use it as per your need. I won't be able to serve hot water to you. But . . . the old man was about to say something, but he held his words back and became silent.

We felt apprehensive. What if the man suddenly changed his mind? We would be in trouble once again.

Rathikant and I blurted out together, "We are extremely grateful to you for this help! This room is just perfect. We couldn't have expected anything better."

"Where is your luggage?" asked the old man.

"Everything is inside our car. Two of our companions are waiting inside the car too. We will go and bring one of them here," replied Rathikant.

"What would you eat at night? I don't have any arrangements for food," said the old man.

"There is absolutely no need for that, so please don't bother," I replied hastily. "We will buy something from the bazaar. Thank you once again for your kindness."

Within the next half an hour, Rathikant, Nathu, and I made ourselves comfortable on the carpet. Ramdeen insisted and stayed back inside the vehicle. Rathikant was extremely tired and I put out the lights so that he could go to sleep. Later, I went out onto the balcony to look around.

The road through the bazaar, which went past the little hilltop, had gradually descended into the adjacent valley. The small wooden house, belonging to the old Jat man, was situated in the alpine valley. As I stood and looked around, the soft cool moonlight slowly flooded in the house with its silvery hue. Along the slope of the valley, across the woods of oak and *chinar*[14], the moonlight created a gorgeous portrait of Mother Nature's abundance. I stood there and beheld that wild and boundless beauty.

The wind carried a biting chill. Yet, my eyes remained devoid of sleep. I didn't feel like sleeping. My heart yearned to stay awake throughout the night and witness the ravishing beauty of the alpine wilderness that surrounded the small wooden house beside the serene valley. However, my body wasn't ready for that nocturnal escapade, as it was too tired after traveling for an entire day. Hence, I was left with no other choice but to lie down and take some rest. And, as soon as I did, I fell asleep.

Much later in the night, my sleep was disrupted by a sudden noise. When I woke up, the noise was still audible, and I felt inquisitive. I got up quickly and went out onto the balcony. When I reached there, my eyes fell upon the woods in the valley. And the sight froze me into a stone. The moon was near the western horizon and in its bright silvery hue, I clearly saw a radiant feminine figure who was riding on a swing from a twisted branch of a tree!

I was stunned. I tried taking a closer look. It was indeed a girl and a very beautiful one. She was perhaps twenty-two or twenty-three years old and was gorgeous to look at. Her ravishing beauty, her oozing sensuality, and her mesmerizing eyes were so attractive that it captivated me with an irresistible charm. However, the hour of the night and the place where she was riding the swing, seemed unbelievable. It was unreal. I had been to Kashmir several times but I couldn't believe any girl of that region would ride a swing in the middle of the wild woods, that too on such a wintry night. It was surreal.

---

[14] Chinar trees, also known as Chinese Banyan, are deciduous trees that belong to the cold regions of the world, mainly in the Kashmir Valley.

Was it a beautiful sight? Certainly, it was. Then why was I feeling an uncanny discomfort? I felt as if there was something in that sight that was creepy, that didn't follow the laws of nature, and was the opposite of reality as it carried a paranormal vibe!

Without wasting a moment, I went inside and called Rathikant. He woke up hurriedly and came out with me onto the balcony. The gorgeous girl with the radiant glow was still riding the swing and seemed totally unaware of everything that surrounded her.

"Who is she?" I asked Rathikant.

He too was dumbfounded by the strange sight. He rubbed his eyes and whispered, "Indeed . . ."

"Is it normal for girls of this region to do such a thing?" I asked again.

"I don't know," murmured Rathikant, "but this is so strange!"

Then, Rathikant suddenly shuddered and shrieked, "Oh goodness! What is that? That swing doesn't have any strings attached to it! Then, how is it hanging from the branches? It is impossible!"

With an equal shock, I looked at the girl and took an closer look. Rathikant was correct. The tree was not far from the wooden house and the moonlight was bright enough for us to notice even if the swing was attached by a thin wire. But no! There was nothing. Nothing connected the swing with any of the branches of the tree. The surreal ride upon the ghostly swing by that uncanny girl was unfolding in front of our eyes. Her radiant glow gave her a ghostly look.

As if this wasn't enough, the entire incident was taking place in complete silence. The whole episode was like an otherworldly nocturnal portrait that had creepily come alive in front of our eyes in the middle of that cursed night. It was like a shadowy portrait of the supernatural.

Rathikant fumbled, "Should we call the old man?"

"Yes, call him," I whispered back. My throat felt dry due to a sudden shiver of fear.

"What if she turns out to be an acquaintance of his? He might get furious," said Rathikant.

"Whatever it is," I said in an irritated voice. "Please go and call him. We shall tackle the matter accordingly."

Within those few moments, while we were talking, we became a little inattentive. The next moment, as we looked back, the girl and the swing were gone! Both had vanished into thin air. There was absolutely nothing under the tree. The twisted branch was still conspicuous in the moonlight, but the beautiful girl and her swing had evaporated.

"Look!" howled Rathikant in a low voice, "Where is the girl and the swing?"

In that bright moonlight, it was impossible for anyone to escape our sight and disappear within those few seconds humanly. Moreover, where would she go? There was only one path, the one that went toward the bazaar. Due to the absence of bushy overgrowths in that alpine woodland, the land under the trees was visible too. It was impossible for anybody to hide from our sight. The entire episode seemed like an impossible supernatural phenomenon!

"What do you think is happening here?" asked Rathikant in an apprehensive voice.

"I don't know!" I said, "I am too puzzled to seek any explanation."

"This is so surrel! What to do now?" he asked.

"Let us get inside and go to sleep," I said grimly, "it is useless to probe further into the matter."

The night was almost over. We slept for an hour or so and then woke up. Nathu was still fast asleep. We woke him up and asked him to pack up our belongings. Then, Rathikant and I went out onto the balcony. That tree in the woods, with its twisted branch, stood in the same place. That morning, it seemed very normal amid the entire woodland. As we stood there in the blatant bright sunlight, everything that we had witnessed the previous night seemed like a nightmare . . . was it though? Was it a nightmare or a sensuous dream? Was it a sensuous dream or a captivating one to hypnotize our senses? Neither Rathikant nor I had any answers for those puzzling questions.

We bid farewell to the old Jat man and went up to our car that was parked at the bazaar. The teashop owner, who had helped us the previous night, was busy igniting his clay stove. He saw us and said, "Hello, Sahib. Hope you slept well last night?"

We replied, "Yes."

The man looked at us suspiciously, even though he didn't express it explicitly, and asked, "I hope nothing unpleasant happened?"

The tone of his voice and the uneasiness in his eyes were clear indicators of an inner fear. We took the tea from him, sat on the wooden bench in front of his shop, and asked him to sit with us. Then, I slowly revealed everything that Rathikant and I witnessed the previous night. I told him everything in detail while he listened carefully.

As I finished, the man smiled sardonically and said, "I know, Babu, I know. That is why I was reluctant to send you to that house at first. Within that mysterious woodland, amid the uncanny silvery hue of the moonlight, many have seen that beautiful girl with her irresistible and captivating beauty. Sahib, she is not a real woman. She is a paranormal creature. She is a djinn, or an *afreet*[15] or maybe a *houri*[16] . . ."

Saying so, he began to move his hand across his entire body, trying to brush away every spec of the ominous thought. Then, he added, "Babu Please leave Kohala immediately. I know many

---

[15] In Arabian and Muslim mythology, afreet is considered a powerful djinn or demon.
[16] In Islamic religious belief, houris are women with beautiful eyes described as a reward for the faithful Muslim men in Paradise.

men who have been hypnotized by the mesmerizing beauty of that she-demon and have stayed back in that wooden house day after day! In their obsessive compulsion, they rented the rooms in that house for indefinite periods, just to be captivated more by her uncanny sensuousness. Eventually, all those men became mad! Their misfortune dragged them into lunacy. One of those ill-fated men even committed suicide. Babu, don't stay here any longer or else your lives too will be in danger. That is the reason why the old Jat man had stopped renting the rooms in his house."

His words were strewn with the apprehension of unknown horror. I asked, "Don't the residents of the village like you see her?"

He replied, "Babu , you don't get to see creatures of the abyss, like the djinn, afreet or a houri every night. That is not possible. There is no rule about the occurrence of those horrific phenomena. However, there is one rule—it must be a bright moonlit night, and the hour has to be the last few ones before dawn. Only in such ominous instances do these beings of the paranormal world come to visit the secluded woodlands. We, the local people of this village, avoid treading the path through the woods, which passes by that wooden house, after nightfall."

Was this man telling us the truth? Or was he trying to scare us? Who was that mysterious and beautiful girl? What did she want? Was she really an houri or a djinn whose dangerous attraction drives human beings to insanity and to their own doom?

There was no way we could find answers to those questions. What we had witnessed with our own eyes was enough for us to trust the words of heed. So, we cleared our dues, boarded our car, and drove away.

***

The Sword of Ronkini Devi

Many things happen in life that don't have any logical explanation. We often label them paranormal or supernatural incidents. Maybe, if we ever know how to seek the reasons behind such events, then it would lead us to a natural and simple explanation. Perhaps such explanations are beyond the perception of human senses and rationale. So, I won't delve deeper into a retrospection. It is best to state that ordinary men and women like us are not equipped enough to explore those unknown terrains. Hence, we label such experiences as paranormal or supernatural ones.

Once, I experienced such an incident and I have never been able to find any logical explanation behind it. Today, I shall reveal that story to my readers and leave it to their own discretions to find a tangible logic behind it. I would be more than happy if anybody could do so.

The incident happened a few years ago. At that time, I was a teacher at the Minor School of a village named Chero in the Manbhum district. The natural beauty of the Chero Village was fascinating. Within a few days of living there, nobody was bound to find any other village across the vast monotonous plains of Bengal as dull and boring. Along the slope of a hill, the entire village was spread across the tableland leading to it. From the houses at the perimeter of the slope, one could easily see the hilltop with thin woods of sal, mahua, and kurchi trees, the big banyan tree with a platform underneath it, numerous small and large boulders, and an abundant overgrowth of thorn bushes.

One evening, I was walking past the village and went up the hill. I was surprised to see the remains of a dilapidated stone-built temple beside the woods at that hilltop. With me were two boys from school. They belonged to the Bengali families of Manbhum. Most of the residents of Chero were from South India, but almost every one of them was fluent in their Bengali accents and some had even adapted many cultural practices too.

The temple was built of black-colored stones and had a peculiar shape. I had never seen a temple with such a shape in that region of Manbhum. It had a strange resemblance to the Dus-Mahavidya temple of the Chachra Palace. It seemed strange because the temple looked out of place amid the designs of any other temple in that district. Moreover, the temple was totally deserted and didn't have an idol of a god or goddess inside it. The stones of the southern wall had started to sink and a part of it had fallen off. There were no doors and just a wrecked stony doorsill could be spotted amid the ruins. Inside that ruined temple, a wild overgrowth of *tulsi*[17] bushes had crowded the entire place.

To be honest, in the evening's twilight, that decrepit temple, which was devoid of its idol, struck a spasm of fear in my heart. But, despite being an ancient holy place of worship that was now

---

[17] Also known as holy basil. Hindus worship this sacred plant as an avatar of goddess Lakshmi.

abandoned, what was it about the temple ruins that instilled a sense of fear deep within me? I wasn't able to find the answer. However, I felt a gripping urge to take a closer look at it and was drawn toward it.

But one of the students stopped and cautioned me, "Sir, please don't go there."

"Why?" I asked with surprise.

"It is not safe to go there," he replied with apprehension. "After dark, the place is said to be infested with snakes. Moreover, people say that the place is infamous for the elusive dangers of the known as well as the unknown. There is a shadow of evil omen around it."

"Is it a temple?" I inquired.

"Sir, this is the temple of goddess Ronkini Devi," he replied in a gloomy voice. "However, even the eldest members of our village haven't seen anybody perform puja in it. The temple was abandoned long ago. Even the idol had gone missing!. The ruins of the temple have remained neglected amid this forest much before the times of our grandfathers. Let's go, sir. We must return to the village now."

The boy was clearly scared and was in a hurry to get back, so I didn't resist. After coming back to the village, I spoke with a few elderly villagers about the matter, too. Strangely, each of them tried to avoid such a discussion. Perhaps, it was my strong intuition; somehow, they were scared to talk about that temple. Hence, I decided not to probe further into the matter.

A year went by. There weren't many students in the school. My workload as a teacher wasn't much as well. During my leisure time, I began to roam around across the region, in different villages and localities, while I collected antiques like old scriptures and artefacts. It had been a hobby of mine, but amid the prolonged periods of leisure time in Chero Village, it became an addiction.

Joychandi Hills were about five miles away from Chero Village. Atop a steep and weird-looking hill, there was a temple of goddess

Joychandi. During the month of *Pous*[18], the place becomes abuzz with its annual springtime carnival. Not far from the Joychandi Hills was a small hamlet which was inhabited by a few Brahmin families from Orissa. It was called the Joychandi Village. Amid the locals of that village, I became quite well acquainted with an old Brahmin named Chandra Mohan Panda. In a typical broken Bengali accent, he used to tell me many interesting stories. During my excursions around Joychandi Hills for antics and scriptures, I used to spend some time with him, listening to his vivid tales of the region.

Chandra Mohan was also the Postmaster of the local post office. His fascinating tales comprised stories of snakes, ghosts, tigers (since the forests were infamous for those notorious beasts) and I was always left enthralled while I listened to them during the uncountable monsoon afternoons I spent in his company. The aura of those stories was like an invisible magnetic force that pulled me toward him.

Those vast and wild woodlands of Manbhum district were far away from the rules of the modern civilized world. The lifestyle in those regions was aloof and independent. Despite the strangeness under the shadows of the Joychandi Hills, inside the little hamlet surrounded by the woods of sal trees, the tales of old Chandra Mohan Panda seemed very real. It felt as if in those mysterious forestlands, such unnatural tales followed some equally mysterious laws of nature, even though they might apparently appear to be bizarre for a man who had lived in the modern city of Kolkata.

During one such afternoon, as I sat and listened to him, Chandra Mohan said, "Have you seen the temple of Ronkini Devi atop the Chero Hills?"

His words surprised me, and I kept staring at him. Till then, I didn't hear anything about the place from anybody else, apart from

---

[18] Pous is the ninth month in the Bengali calendar; it marks the start of winter.

that little conversation I had with one of the students when I last visited the Chero Hills.

I replied, "Yes, I did visit it once. However, every single person, whom I had asked about Ronkini Devi, had either avoided the discussion or had diverted the subject to something else."

"Every one of them is afraid of Ronkini Devi," replied Chandra Mohan.

"But why?" I asked,

Chandra Mohan said, "Long ago, the region of Manbhum was inhabited by savage tribal races. Ronkini Devi was a goddess who was predominantly worshiped by those people. With time, Hindu families came to live in these lands and their population became more predominant. So, with the natural progression of time, she became a Hindu goddess. Then, some of those people built that temple atop the hill. However, it must not be forgotten that Ronkini Devi is unlike any other Hindu goddess. She is a deity of the wild savage races! In those ancient times, human sacrifice was performed at that temple. Even sixty years ago, that practice existed."

I sat speechless and listened while Chandra Mohan continued, "There is an ancient belief that an inevitable catastrophe strikes whenever Ronkini Devi is displeased. Her wrath holds such immense power that it unleashes a deluge of omens and death upon all those living in the region! It has happened many times and has sealed the belief in the hearts of the people. Legend has it that before every devastating epidemic that plagued these lands, the sacrificial sword in the hands of Ronkini Devi's idol would be mysteriously coated in blood, a belief deeply ingrained in the hearts of every inhabitant in these regions. About forty years ago, when I had just relocated here, I had heard this story from the residents."

"Did you see the idol of Ronkini Devi?" I asked.

"No," replied Chandra Mohan, "when I came here, the temple was in the same ruined state. It was fabled that some invaders from a distant land had taken away her idol long ago. I had heard stories about Ronkini Devi from a descendant of the ancient worshipers of that temple when I was young. He used to live in the Chero Village. I visited his house several times. He was the one who told me about the myth of Ronkini Devi's sacrificial sword getting smeared in blood. The descendants of those worshipers don't exist anymore. It has been years since I last visited Chero Village. I am an old man now, and I have stopped going out much."

"What was the idol of Ronkini Devi like?" I questioned.

"I had heard that it had the form of goddess *Kali*," he replied. "Back in the ancient ages of savagery, it was fabled that a real sacrificial severed human head used to hang from one of her hands! Legends say that uncountable human sacrifices have taken place at that temple. Amid the woods, there is a mound behind the temple which still exists. If it is dug, even now you might find a few skulls buried under it."

The Legend of Ronkini Devi was a daunting one—no doubt why the locals feared her wrath. I must admit that when I went back to my house in Chero from Joychandi Village shivers of fear ran down my spine as I walked across the vast wilderness that evening.

Then, two more years went by . . .

It is true that the natural beauty of Chero Village and its surroundings mesmerized me so much that I intended to stay there for many more years. However, soon a scuffle began to brew in the school between the Bengali and the South Indian communities. The latter were much more benevolent in their financial aid to the school, and they started to flex their muscles over the reins of the school's administration. They demanded that people from their communities should have a majority in the school's governing committee. They even demanded to employ an English teacher from South India only. Contrastingly, as I was the sole teacher of

English in that school, the brawl became a threat to my own job. With time, the matter became so serious that it was difficult for me to save my position in the school.

I recalled that a high school had been built at a place closer to my hometown. Earlier, due to the fear of predominant cases of malaria, I ignored their request to employ me. However, at that time, with no other option at hand, I wrote to them for an employment opportunity. Despite everything, that was not the reason why I was compelled to leave Chero Village. Then, why did I leave? Well, I will reveal that later.

Later, one morning, Chandra Mohan Panda came to visit Chero Village. I was thrilled by the news and requested him to visit my house for a cup of tea and spend some time with me. I literally arrested him and his bullock cart and took him home.

Old Chandra Mohan had never been to my place in Chero Village. However, as he entered, he looked around in amazement and asked me, "Do you live in this house?"

I replied, "Yes. It is a small village and there are not many options to rent a house. Earlier, I used to live in a room within the school's building. A year ago, Raghunath, the school's secretary, arranged this house for me. I live here alone, all by myself."

Honestly, I was lucky enough to get that house. With its old and strong stone masonry structure, three large rooms, and one sprawling veranda, the house was robust. One could easily proclaim it to be a small fortress of the medieval era. Many powerful earthquakes too possibly didn't have the strength to even damage it.

Old Chandra Mohan sat inside the house and started to look around closely with a strange interest. I thought perhaps he was fascinated by the robust architecture of the house. I added, "The house is a very hardy! With its ancient stone masonry, it is still strong enough to endure the tides of time . . ."

"No, I am not thinking that. It is something else," replied Chandra Mohan, as if he was in a trance, "I have visited this house earlier. About thirty years ago, I was a regular visitor at this place . . . Yes, now I recall everything! This house once belonged to the family of Ronkini Devi's worshipers. I didn't know you lived here. Well, it is such a pleasant surprise! It is so wonderful that it gives me goosebumps. I have come to this house after so many years."

Gradually, our discussion floated toward other topics. Then, after having some tea and some refreshments, Chandra Mohan went away on his bullock cart.

Another year passed. Meanwhile, I received confirmation of employment from the high school closer to my hometown, but I had not yet decided to go. The scuffle between the Bengali and the South Indian communities had mellowed down, and I didn't lose my job. So, I decided to stay in the village longer.

Soon, it was the end of the month of Chaitra. One day, I got an invitation to attend the Annapurna Puja festivities at a student's ancestral house which was in a village a few miles away. It was a weekend, so I hired a bullock cart on Saturday to visit their house. I had planned to spend the next two days at their place. I returned to Chero on Tuesday afternoon. I had taken Rakhohori with me for the trip as a help. He used to work as a cleaner in the school and had great admiration for me.

As we returned, Rakhohori unlocked the door of my house and shrieked, "Oh . . . whose blood is that? Babu, come and look!"

I was astounded. I jumped out of the bullock cart and went to take a closer look. Rakhohori was correct. The blood went from a corner of the front door's threshold, down the courtyard, inside the house. It wasn't in a continuous flow, though. It was a sinewy line of blood drops scattered closely. However, it was evidently fresh blood, as if a severed human head had just been carried along that path while fresh blood dripped down along the way.

I was speechless. Whose blood was it? Where did so much blood come from?

To unravel a plausible explanation, my thoughts sifted through countless possibilities. Was it the blood of an animal? Perhaps a cat, a dog, a rodent, or a rat? I tried to seek an answer, and it was the closest possible reasoning.

I asked Rakhohori, "Can you find out where the blood is coming from? I am sure this is the deed of that big cat of this locality."

Rakhohori did as I said and soon discovered that the flow had gone down the staircase and then toward the threshold of a small room below the stairs. We felt skeptical and followed it. The room was a tiny, dark, and unused one. It had been stacked with old and discarded furniture and I never bothered to go inside it ever since I started to live in that house. As we stood outside, it was evident that the stream of blood droplets was coming from inside the room. However, it seemed so very unreal. That day, for the first time, we entered that room, whose door had been locked for ages.

I wondered, "Even if this is a deed of that notorious cat, how could it enter the room through this locked door?"

Rakhohori broke the iron lock and chain with a shovel. Then, we took a lantern and went inside. The dingy room was filled with broken cupboards, tin boxes, old torn mattresses, rotten wooden furniture, and many other unused and discarded things. We looked at the floor and saw that the drops of blood were going in a particular direction.

Rakhohori shrieked, "Babu, this is impossible! How could the blood droplets emerge from here?"

He picked something up and said in a surprised tone, "Babu, come and take a look! Come see what I found."

I ran up to him to find out, but what I saw froze me with a

astonishment. It was an old and rusted *Rāmdāo*[19]! The hilt of the sword was missing, the shape of the blade was curved near the top, and it had a tapered width near the bottom. However, the most baffling thing was the sight of fresh blood that was dripping from the entire sharp side of the Rāmdāo!

I stood there speechless while a gust of memories rushed in and crowded my mind. They were memories of what Chandra Mohan Panda had said two years ago. He said that the house where I lived belonged to the family of Ronkini Devi's worshipers. *Was it then Ronkini Devi's own sacrificial sword? Was this Rāmdāo used to be in the hand of her idol at her legendary temple atop Chero Hill?'* My mind was crowded with questions and an unknown fear!

I tried to seek a reason and my mind answered my soul . . . *'Perhaps, when the idol was taken away from the temple, the family of her worshipers kept that sword hidden inside this dingy room.'*

Then, I remembered the myth . . . *'Before every catastrophic epidemic that had plagued the lands of Manbhum, the sacrificial sword in the hands of Ronkini Devi's idol used to become magically smeared in blood!'*

The sudden recollection of the horrific truth made me feel dizzy. Shivers ran down my spine, I felt I was searching for an unknown nemesis in the darkness!

When and where will the epidemic strike? The question was simple, but I didn't get enough time to ask it to myself and do something about it.

The next evening brought in the shocking news of the first case of cholera in Chero Village. It was the harbinger of death. Within the next three days, the epidemic had spread its wings across the region—first Chero, then the adjacent Kajra Village, and then the next and then the next. The deathly shroud of cholera covered and consumed everything. The force of death dealt a fatal blow,

---

[19] A sacrificial sword.

leaving scarcely any survivors among the South Indian inhabitants of Chero.

As the school was closed for an indefinite period, I took the first opportunity and fled back home. I never returned to Chero Village again. Before the upcoming summer vacations, I took up a new job at the high school that was at a place closer to my hometown.

Some questions remained ingrained in my mind, perhaps forever . . .

Was Ronkini Devi really a goddess who had always informed mortals about an impending calamity?

Could the natives or the modern residents ever unearth the truth?

Despite that, ever since that incident, I have continued to harbor a reverence for the mystic goddess Ronkini Devi and her sacrificial sword.

***

The Ancestral Home

The colossal brick-built house stood silently by the banks of the rippling Madhumati River. On the veranda, which faced the river, Radhamohan sat upon a chair and tried to read a book. However, his mind failed to focus, and he was unable to read. The wandering subconscious mind of Radhamohan floated from the pages of the book toward the untamed beauty that surrounded him.

In front of his eyes was the beautiful rural landscape through which the sparkling water of the rivulet was flowing down silently. Woods of bamboo and mango crowded together with their surplus of green hues on the opposite. Perhaps, it was once a proper mango garden, but over the years, it had become a dense woodland.

Radhamohan enjoyed staying alone in that huge house, which once belonged to his ancestors. The quiet, tranquil vastness of his ancestral home had a serene peacefulness in it. Radhamohan loved that soft serenity. Once inhabited by his ancestors, the house was now completely empty. After the family went away to the city, nobody lived in or visited it anymore. That day, in that absorbing calmness, Radhamohan thought of enjoying his leisure hours while reading a good book or indulging in penning down some creative lines of his own.

Years ago, his father, Shyamakant Chakraborty, had left the village while he was in his teens. He moved in with his maternal uncle's family, who used to live in Midnapore. There, Shyamakant completed his education and became a lawyer. Gradually, he moved up the ladder of success and became a wealthy lawyer. He had built his own house in Midnapore and he lived there with his family. He did make a few occasional visits to his ancestral home, maybe once or twice, but didn't stay there for long. He was a busy man; he couldn't afford to stay away from his work. Even the other relatives, who once lived in that house, had moved out gradually in search of better prospects of making a good living. The old house has persisted like a frail old lady, reaping memories of the yesteryears.

Radhamohan graduated as a lawyer too recently, and had busied himself in managing the flourishing legal business that his deceased father had left behind. Amid all the pangs of the busy and prosperous lifestyle of the family, the ancestral lands and the huge empty house continued to drown in neglectful obscurity. But something needed to be done about it too. So, as soon as Radhamohan received the letter from his village about looking after their ancestral inheritance, he visited his ancestral home during Durga Puja holidays, and planned to sell off the lands and the property before the deserted house turned into ruins.

As Radhamohan arrived in the village, the neighbors embraced him with warmth. Old Bhairav Barua, who lived in the adjacent house, took care of Radhamohan in his household. With the sheer force of his loving hospitality, Bhairav Barua had taken great care of every meal ever since Radhamohan had arrived. Radhamohan felt overwhelmed by it and couldn't refuse Bhairav's caring cordiality.

As Radhamohan sat with a smile on his face and pondered over his experiences, Bhairav's son, Keshto, came and asked, "Dada, would you like to have some tea? Come with me . . ."

Radhamohan interrupted and said, "Keshto, can you bring it here? I just don't want to go from this place. The beauty of the evening twilight by the river is so beautiful. I want to sit here quietly for some more time and seep in this beauty."

Keshto smiled and replied, "Really, Dada? Alright, I will get it for you quickly."

It was not just Bhairav Barua's family, but almost every villager had extended their love and care toward Radhamohan. The elderly men had said with sympathy, "You are Shyamakant's son, so you are a son of this soil too. How can we let you cook your own meals while you're visiting your ancestral house after such a long time? These few days, we will take care of all your needs."

Radhamohan felt grateful. The villagers, men, and women of the same soil where his ancestors had grown up and lived, were too affectionate.

Within a few minutes, Keshto came back with the tea, gave it to Radhamohan, and went away. Once again, Radhamohan sat alone in that serene evening and watched the day fade into the night as it covered everything around with a silken dark veil. In that darkness, he could see the reflection of the vast starlit sky upon the clear water of the Madhumati River.

Radhamohan sat and wondered, "Why did my great-grandfather build this house in this remote village? During his lifetime, he was a valiant *Daroga*[20] of the Police Department. He had made a fortune during his lifetime, but he was perhaps naïve in worldly affairs. Or else, why would a man of wealth like him come to a remote village and spend money to build such a huge house? Sadly, the property

---

[20] A chief officer.

that he had once built with his brimming fortune is of no use now to his descendants. Oh, what a waste."

He contemplated, "What if the brick masons buy the house? In that case, the house can be sold off brick by brick for a price . . ."

His thoughts were interrupted by a sudden knock at the door. Radhamohan turned around and saw a little girl, about ten or eleven years old, standing behind the door and looking at him. Her fair and innocent face had a subtle shyness mingled with hesitation while she peeped from that semi-dark corner. The room adjacent to the veranda, where Radhamohan was sitting, was fairly illuminated by the light of the lantern. A part of that light fell near the door too and made her visible.

Radhamohan wondered, "Bhairav Barua is so cordial. Once he comes himself, on another occasion, he sent his son to look after me. Now, he has sent his little daughter to check if I need anything."

He asked softly, "Hello there, is the dinner prepared already?"

The girl came forward a bit hesitantly and stood silently in the light.

Radhamohan smiled at her and asked, "What is your name?"

She replied softly, "Lokhhi."

"It is a beautiful name," said Radhamohan, "Do you go to school?"

"No," she replied.

"Can you sing?" asked Radhamohan.

"No," she replied.

"Well, then things would be a bit complicated while arranging for your marriage," smiled Radhamohan, "How about cooking? Do you know how to cook?"

The girl nodded her head in agreement.

Radhamohan said, "Good! That is a great talent. What all can you cook?"

"Everything," replied the girl.

"Everything?" said Radhamohan, "Wow! You're a nice girl. Come, sit down."

She nodded her head shyly and replied, "No, I won't sit."

"Why? Do you have any work to do?" asked Radhamohan.

"No," she replied again.

"Well then, please sit," said Radhamohan while turning his head toward the veranda.

"No, I will go now," she replied softly, "You go and have your dinner."

"Yes, I will. Have they finished cooking?" Radhamohan asked.

"You're feeling very hungry, right? Go, and hake your dinner. It is ready I guess," she answered.

Radhamohan wanted to ask something, but as he turned back, the girl was gone. He felt a bit odd but didn't pay much heed. Then, he went to Bhairav Barua's house for dinner.

As he reached, Bhairav welcomed him and said, "Come my dear, dinner is almost ready."

Radhamohan replied, "Yes. Your daughter came to inform me about it."

After dinner, Radhamohan went back to his ancestral home. He was all alone in that huge house, but Radhamohan enjoyed the serene tranquility. As he reclined on his bed, he could feel the reminiscences of his bygone forefathers in the darkness of the beautiful moonlit night. It was as though he could hear their footsteps and their cheerful murmur all around him. His grandfather had spent the beautiful days of his childhood in that house. His grandmother had stepped into that house as a newlywed bride. After so many years and after garnering so many precious memories, their descendants had left behind everything and had migrated to far-off lands in the cities. Therefore, that beautiful ancestral home gradually became estranged from them while they drifted away from their roots.

As Radhamohan was absorbed in deep sleep, the remnant energies of his forefathers perhaps came and murmured into his ears . . . *Why did you leave us behind? Why did our children abandon us? What was our mistake that all of you deserted and left us alone in this village? In this huge house, we long for one glimpse of our beloved family with all our love . . .*

The next morning, Radhamohan woke up and became busy finalizing the land and property deals. The day went by and then in the evening, Radhamohan came back to his ancestral home. He freshened up and then sat on a chair on the veranda.

The night was dark but tranquil, and Radhamohan sat and rested quietly. Somewhere, there was a light tapping sound, but Radhamohan didn't notice it. Silently, the little girl once again came and stood by the door.

Suddenly, Radhamohan noticed her and said in surprise, "Is that you?"

"Hmmm," came her reply.

"Is the dinner ready?" he asked.

"It would be a bit late tonight. They are cooking mutton . . . especially for you," she said.

"Oh wow!" replied Radhamohan, "That means tonight there would be a great feast."

The girl smiled a little and then became quiet. Radhamohan felt content. He wondered . . . *She is such a nice little girl. She speaks so nicely and softly while her nature is so calm and composed . . .*

He asked her, "Where does your maternal family belong to?"

"I have forgotten," she said sadly.

"Why? Don't you visit their place?" asked Radhamohan.

The girl nodded her head softly and replied indifferently, "No."

Radhamohan felt amused at her nonchalant and carefree attitude.

She asked, "Have you come here alone? Bring the ladies of the family with you too. This is such a huge house of yours, but it remains deserted and devoid of the people who truly belong here. Bring them with you. They would love to be here."

"Is that your wish too?" asked Radhamohan with a smile.

"It is indeed, very much!" she replied.

"Why?" asked Radhamohan.

"For ages, this house has been like this. For ages, it has been all alone. For ages, nobody has come here to live. There is no one who would light a lamp in the evening." she continued.

Radhamohan felt surprised by the sensitive words of that little girl. Whatever she confessed was very pertinent and nostalgic.

Radhamohan asked smilingly, "And, you feel bad about it. Isn't it?"

"Yes, why not?" she replied with vigor, "You should come here with the family, with the ladies of the household. Once again, this beautiful house would throb with life. It would vibrate with the sounds of the conch. The women would light the lamps every evening. Don't you think this ancestral house of yours deserves that domestic bliss?"

She finished her words and then said hurriedly, "Oh, you must be very hungry. Isn't it? It is getting late."

"No, don't worry, my dear," replied Radhamohan affectionately. "It is not that late in the night."

"I know, you have a habit of eating early," she added.

"How do you know that little girl?" asked Radhamohan with surprise.

She giggled without answering and stood there shyly.

A few moments later, she nodded her head happily and said with a smile, "Yes . . . I really love it. I really love it."

"What is it that you love?" asked Radhamohan.

She replied gleefully, "I love it when this house buzzes with life. I feel happy when it becomes inhabited by its true family. Like now, when you have come. I really love it."

She paused a bit and added, "Now go. The mutton is ready. Please hurry up. Go and have your dinner. They are waiting for you."

"How do you know that the mutton is ready?" asked Radhamohan inquisitively.

"I know it, believe me," she replied confidently. "Now go and have your dinner."

"Wait, let me first go and wash my face and my hands. Then, we will go together," said Radhamohan.

Saying so, Radhamohan got up and went inside. However, when he returned, she was gone. In that blend of darkness and the lantern's light, he couldn't see her anywhere.

Radhamohan sighed and thought, 'Well, she is a little child with a restless heart; she couldn't resist to wait any longer. But she has such a pure heart, and she is so chirpy and funny. I like her childish innocence."

As Radhamohan reached Bhairav Barua's house, he said humbly, "Please come inside. I was about to send somebody to ask you to come. I apologize for the delay tonight. We have got some mutton for dinner. You have accepted our hospitality and we are happy that we extended our bit to you. But we have been able to provide you with casual meals only. So, I thought that we must do something special for you, at least, for a night's dinner."

Radhamohan felt embarrassed and replied shyly, "No, uncle, what are you saying? Please don't bother about the meals. I am like one of your own children and please don't worry. I am not a stranger in this household. I feel so happy and blessed by the love and care of this entire family."

That night went away happily and so did the next day. Then, in the evening, after twilight, Lokhhi came to visit Radhamohan once again.

Radhamohan saw her and said, "Lokhhi, is that you? Come, I was just thinking about you."

"Really?" asked Lokhhi with a laugh.

"Yes, believe me. I was indeed thinking about you," said Radhamohan.

Lokhhi nodded her head childishly and said, "I know what you were thinking about me."

"You know?" asked Radhamohan.

"Yes, I know it," she added, "But, I won't tell it to you."

Radhamohan had bought some *sandesh*[21] to surprise her. To be precise, that afternoon, he had asked Hari Nandi's maid, Amulya, to get it from the Islamhati Bazaar, which was famous for its sandesh sweetshops. Radhamohan was annoyed with Amulya for probably leaking his little secret to Lokhhi and spoiling his plans to surprise her.

Nonetheless, with a faint ray of hope, Radhamohan added, "No, I don't think you know it. Well, if you know it, then tell me, what is it?"

She smiled softly and said, "I know it."

There was a subtle composure in her voice that made Radhamohan not question her any further. He, too, understood that she knew. It reflected clearly in her warm smile.

Radhamohan muttered, "Amulya is a hopeless fellow. Did he have to spill the beans? He couldn't even retain one simple thing with himself!"

She laughed and said, "Alright, now give me the sandesh!"

Radhamohan got up to fetch the sandesh, but as he returned, she was gone! He felt surprised by her sudden acts of appearances and disappearances. He sighed, "How strange! She is such a restless little girl. She just ran away within these few moments."

That night, during dinnertime, Radhamohan took the sandesh along with him to Bhairav Barua's house. He gave it to him and

---

[21] A delicious Bengali sweet.

said, "This is for your little girl. She is very shy, and she went away before I could offer it to her. Can you give it to her?"

Bhairav Barua laughed and said, "Did she come to meet you?"

"Yes," replied Radhamohan, "In fact, she visits me daily. We sit together and chat."

"Really?" said Bhairav Barua, "Well, she is a little chirpy, but she is indeed a bit shy."

The next evening, as the twilight faded away, Lokhhi came and stood at her usual place on the veranda.

Radhamohan looked at her and said, "Why did you suddenly go away last evening? You know, I got very annoyed."

She smiled a little and stood without saying anything.

Radhamohan asked again, "Did you have the sandesh?"

She replied, "Why not? In fact, I was already savoring the sandesh when you mentioned it to me!"

Before Radhamohan could interpret her words, she added, "See, I am so happy nowadays! After you arrived here, this house has come alive once again. The lamps are lit every evening. The air has a freshness of life and the house has the company of one whose roots truly belong here. Yes, it is you and your presence makes all the difference. Otherwise, it feels so lonely here."

"Would you come to the city?" asked Radhamohan, "Come with me. I will take you there."

"No, I like it here," she said, "I don't want to go to the city."

Radhamohan tried to convince her, "Why not? There is so much fun in the city. There are talkies and cinemas! There is good food and so many good places to visit."

"These pleasures don't interest me and I don't care about them," she replied, "tell me, will you come again? Promise, me that you will."

"Yes, I will definitely come," said Radhamohan, "Why won't I come?"

"For all these days, you never came," she said in a melancholy voice, "this house has stayed alone and been deserted for ages. That is why I am asking. Well, I will go now. I know, you are leaving on Tuesday."

Radhamohan was astonished. Did he tell Bhairav Barua about his plan to return on Tuesday? Did Bhairav discuss it with his family? Radhamohan couldn't recall. Neither could he decipher how Lokhhi got to know it.

Over the next two days, Radhamohan went to finish some urgent work. On Monday night, he returned to his ancestral home. Since it was quite late, he decided not to disturb Bhairav Barua and his family. He finished a quick dinner with some dry snacks at home and went to sleep.

The next morning, Bhairav arrived and asked hurriedly, "When did you return last night? Did you get late? What did you have for dinner? My son, you should have called us. You are like my own child; why did you hesitate?"

Radhamohan apologized shyly and then said, "Can you call your little daughter once?"

Bhairav Barua replied, "Yes, why not? Wait, let me go and call her."

After a while, Bhairav Barua returned with a little girl. She had a dusky complexion and was about eight years old.

Radhamohan looked at the girl, whom he was seeing for the first time, and said, "No, uncle. I was talking about her elder sister."

Bhairav Barua replied in an astonished voice, "But . . . her elder sister is already married. She lives with her husband's family. I don't think you have met her."

Radhamohan was perplexed too. He fumbled, "Then, is there any other little girl in your household?"

Bhairav was confused. He replied, "No, there are no other girls in my house. Well, then . . . is it someone else? But that is impossible.

There are no girls of that age in this tiny neighborhood. Son, tell me something. How old was this girl?"

Radhamohan seemed confused. He looked back at Bhairav and said, "Her name was Lokhhi. She had told me her name herself."

"Lokhhi?" added Bhairav Barua in an even more confused voice, "I bet that there isn't any little girl by the name of Lokhhi in this village. I guess, you must have heard her name incorrectly."

"But, even if I have mistakenly heard the wrong name," said Radhamohan, "who is the girl? Her existence cannot be a mistake!"

"That is what is confusing me!" replied Bhairav Barua, "There are no girls with that name or of that age in our entire neighborhood."

In a state of total confusion, Radhamohan went back to his home. He was unable to understand anything. Moreover, Lokhhi didn't come to visit him after he had returned from his trip to the adjacent village. Everything seemed so perplexing.

*

Two years after returning from his ancestral village, Radhamohan visited his paternal aunt at her house in Jabalpur. The passage of time had almost erased the memories of that strange experience from his mind.

In the humid afternoon, as he was sitting lazily in the living room, his eyes fell on an old photograph inside an old photo album. It was a photograph of a little girl. She seemed very familiar, but Radhamohan was unable to recall who she was.

He took the photograph to his aunt and asked, "Who is this girl? She seems so familiar."

The old lady looked and said, "Oh . . . no, my dear, you haven't ever met her. She was my younger sister. Unfortunately, she died at the tender age of twelve. You weren't even born at that time because your parents were not married then. At that time, we used to live in the village, in our ancestral home."

In a state of melancholy that floated in with a gush of old memories, she too floated away into the past and murmured on her own, "Ah . . . I can still remember her as a little angel. She was so pretty and innocent. I used to love her so much. It's been forty years. After her fateful demise, Baba decided to relocate the entire family to Midnapore. Ever since then, I have never been to that beautiful house in our village. After I got married, it was just once that I visited it. That too was twenty-five years ago."

Radhamohan was speechless. His subconscious mind had by then found what he was trying to recall. He knew who she was, but he sat there motionless while his mind felt dizzy. With a choked voice, he asked, "What was her name?"

His old aunt replied, "Her name was . . . LOKHHI."

***

The Unexplained

It was a stormy evening and our clubhouse at Lichutala Road was abuzz with gossip of the strange and the unreal. However, that routine *adda*[22] mostly comprised tasteless ghost stories. The so-called paranormal stories from rural mango gardens and bamboo hedges were insipid in every manner. The overly familiar image of a horrible ghost standing in the dark, in its customary white drape, had been overfed into our hearts and minds since childhood. Thus, the stories failed to arouse a fresh sense of thrill within us. Moreover, none of us could come up with anything beyond that very familiar paradigm of the paranormal.

Soon, Sharat Chakraborty arrived at our little clubhouse. He was a man who had garnered vast experience in life. After years of working as an employee of the Excise Department, he had recently retired from his job. Sharat Babu was almost sixty

---

[22] Means casual chats or gossips.

years old and was a staunch practitioner of tantric rituals. Practicing astrology was his hobby, and many times, he even prepared horoscopes for his acquaintances without any fee. He was always proactive to help anybody, and everyone respected him. As a sign of their reverence, many people refrained from even smoking in his presence.

Sharat Babu entered and asked, "Well then, what is happening here? What is this evening's prevalent gossip? Ah . . . the rain today is too heavy!"

Shyamapada, the Mukhtar, replied, "Welcome, Sharat Babu. We were discussing ghost stories. The monsoon evening is apt for it, but somehow, we are unable to strike a chord. Well, we all know that in your vast experience, you have . . ."

Sharat Chakraborty interrupted and said, "Well, I can tell a story. But it is not a usual ghost story. Is it a tale of the paranormal? Is it the tale of the incorporeal? That is up to all of you to interpret. I don't know, but I strongly believe that it is a true one."

So, Sharat Chakraborty sat down to narrate the story of a strange experience while we sat and listened to it . . .

*

Many years ago, for a job assignment, I had to spend some months in the Doars region, near Jalpaiguri. At that time, my family was settled in Dhaka. So, I went for the work alone. I was unfamiliar with that new place, and it wasn't possible to relocate my entire family before I had made some arrangements to live there. Moreover, I didn't want to disrupt my children's schooling. They were already attending school in Dhaka.

The place where I had to go was far away from Jalpaiguri. I had to travel by the narrow-gauge railways that went through multiple tea estates and dense forests and then reached my destination.

From that remote place, the snowcapped peaks of the Himalayas were visible beyond the green horizons of the vast woodlands. That extremely remote place was solitarily confined within its own perimeter. The name of the place was Haldia.

The isolated rustic region was comprised of only a handful of human settlements. In that remote habitation, I arrived and took shelter in the Senior Sub-Inspector, Mr Revati Mohan Mukherjee's residence. It was monsoon season, and I had yet to find a house of my own, but he was an extremely amicable and helpful gentleman who took great care of me while I stayed with him in his house. He even helped me to find a house of my own within a few days. The tall and slim Revati Mohan Babu belonged to the Nadia district of Bengal.

On the third day after my arrival, he said to me in the morning, "Can I tell you something?"

"Yes, please. What is it?" I asked.

"You coming here to Haldia, during this time of the year, is not right," he added.

"But why do you think so?" I asked doubtfully.

"Well . . . Sharat Babu, aren't you aware of anything about this place?" he asked in a grim voice.

"No," I replied, "what is the matter?"

"This is the monsoon season, and during this time, the notorious Blackwater fever becomes predominant in this region. You are new to this place, and you would be vulnerable to be infected by a fever. Unfortunately, a recurring fever is a symptom of this fatal disease. In that case, the disease becomes a threat to one's life."

I listened to him and asked, "But how have you and your family been able to survive?"

"I would say that it is a grave misfortune," he repented, "I am not here by choice. I am here for a meager living. It is a matter of survival. If I leave this job and go back, I won't be able to get another job at this age that would support the means of survival for my family. What will I feed them? How will I run the household? Sharat Babu, this devilish fever has already taken away two of my beloved daughters. Even then, the company didn't grant my application for a transfer. So, I am stuck here with my remaining family. It is the verdict of destiny."

"That means . . ." I wanted to say something but was interrupted by Revati Mohan Babu.

He said, "Sharat Babu, try to take every precaution to be safe. That should protect you. Wherever you go, always boil your water before drinking it. Make it a thumb rule for yourself."

I felt anxious and asked, "Does every victim of that fever die?"

"In the absence of good treatment, the chances of survival are faint," he replied, "This is especially the case during monsoons and for people who are new to this place. It becomes very difficult to save them if they are infected with Blackwater fever. I have seen two such cases. Unfortunately, both didn't survive."

The discussion left a cloud of fear in my heart, but how much precaution can one take in a foreign land? It was useless to worry. So, I chose to leave my fate in the hands of destiny and began to focus on my work. Spread across ten or twelve miles around Haldia, I had the task of inspecting local wine and ganja shops. As an employee of the Excise Department, it was my prime job.

Soon, everything began to feel nice. Monsoon's campaign of green vibrancy had already started across the woodlands. The dense forests came alive with the colors of beautiful wildflowers and the chirping songs of innumerable species of wild birds. Beyond those throbbing woods, at times, the snowy Himalayan peaks used to peep out through the clouds. From a distance, they used to appear like sugar-coated mountains from the fairytales which sparkled in sunlight. Nonetheless, sunlight was often subdued by the predominant monsoon clouds.

Soon, with Revati Babu's help, I was able to find a decent home for myself. On a strong wooden platform atop four equally strong wooden planks, it was a bungalow-styled house. The wooden floor protected itself from getting damp. The house was quite spacious and used to get ample amounts of light and air.

Gradually, the elusive fear of the devilish fever began to fade. My heart contemplated, "Perhaps, it wasn't right for Revati Babu to scare me like that. After all, I had just arrived in Haldia, and his words ingrained an elusive fear in my fear. Maybe, it was not the right thing to do."

Then, my mind asked two bizarre questions to my heart and perplexed me further, *But, why did he do that? Did he have any other motive?*

After a few days, I managed to get a bearer of my own. His name was Digambar Pandey. He had been living in Haldia for many years, and he was a good cook too. He started to manage my kitchen and take care of my meals, and I felt much more relieved.

Two months later, as a supervisory inspector, I had to visit a place called Bamanpara North. It was a small bazaar beside a tea estate named Bamanpara North Tea Estate. My bullock cart crossed a small hilly rivulet and arrived at the bazaar at around ten o'clock in the morning. Two Marwari Mahajan had their shops at the bazaar. They were the prime merchants of the region's harvests. A man, named Deven Samanta, had a timber business there. His brother, Sashi Samanta, owned the local ganja and opium shop; I was supposed to audit its accounts. However, destiny had some other plans.

As I sat inside the shop and skimmed through the accounts, I started to feel sick. Then, a severe headache gripped me. Unable to control the discomfort, I informed Deven Samanta of the sudden uneasiness. He gave me a homeopathic medicine and said, "Please don't worry, this medicine will cure you."

I took the medicine and asked warily, "Does Blackwater fever happen here?"

"Yes, it happens a lot," replied Deven.

"Do people die?" I asked in alarm.

"Well, they do . . ." replied Deven dryly.

"Don't you feel scared?" I asked again.

"Babu, we have been residing in this region for a long time. People who are new to this place usually feel scared. We, the existing residents, have adapted to our fears," said Deven.

I couldn't say anything further. Ever since my arrival in Haldia, every person I met had said the same thing whenever I asked them about their fears. So, I tried to focus on my work. However, I soon realized that I was unable to do so as my entire body felt fatigued with every passing moment. Nonetheless, I hurried and completed the remaining work and got into the bullock cart to return. On my way back, I felt so thirsty that I was compelled to stop by a dingy warehouse adjacent to the Bamanpara North Tea Estate and drink some water from its doorkeeper.

By the time I reached Haldia, it was quite late, and my body was shivering with fever. Revati Babu received the news and came running. Soon, the doctor was summoned too. Then, after continuous treatment with medicines and injections over the next three days, my fever finally receded. I sighed in relief as my body recovered from the sudden sickness.

The following two weeks passed without any issues. People around me said, "Perhaps, a sudden bout of common cold was the cause of the fever. There is nothing to worry about."

Their words gave me courage, and I made myself believe the same. So, I focused on my work, and I felt no more trouble with my health.

Then, one evening, as I was sitting at the Haldia Police Station and chatting with the local daroga, the fever came back with a blatant suddenness. Daroga Babu felt concerned and asked his men to take me back home.

I reached and asked Digambar to get me some water. As he fetched it hurriedly, I gulped it down and stretched myself on the bed. For the next three days, I was completely overpowered by the assault of the fever. Revati Babu and Daroga Babu used to visit me twice every day to learn about my recovery and well-being. They even guided Digambar to prepare sago and barley porridge for me. Finally, after three long days, my fever went away, and I gradually regained my strength. It is true that without their care and benevolence, I would've been stranded there.

Soon, I went back to work. However, fifteen days later, while I was doing auditing at a nearby tea estate, I was struck by the fever again. It was strange and I realized that the bouts of fever were like conjuring tricks that came and went away without any indication or reason. So, I felt accustomed to its jugglery. I was very scared the first time I had the fever. However, recurrent assaults of the same sickness had, by then, erased much of that apprehension.

That day, I went back home and asked Digambar to prepare sago and barley porridge for me. It was the only and safest diet for the sick. However, there was something different about the fever this time. Unfortunately, I couldn't understand it right away.

The fever didn't recede so easily. Two days later, I began experiencing all the symptoms of the feared Blackwater fever. Hence, it took almost six long days for me to get cured. Meanwhile, two days after I was afflicted by the fever, Revati Babu and Daroga Babu came to see me. However, when I asked Digambar to make some tea for them, they politely refused to have it. I understood that they too were scared as they probably considered my Blackwater fever to be contagious.

Daroga Babu said to me, "Sharat Babu, can I suggest something?"

I replied, "Yes, please . . ."

He said, "I think you should go back to your home."

"Why would you suggest that?" I asked.

"Well, even the doctor thinks so . . ." he replied.

"But he didn't tell me anything directly," I said.

Daroga Babu hesitated a bit and answered, "No, he didn't. But he insisted that we should tell this to you. He said that the nature of your illness is very severe. I mean . . ."

I interrupted, "But I am recovering well. Am I not?"

"Sharat Babu, recovering from it is not so easy. It is very difficult to do it," he added.

"Very well," I answered, "but with this weakness, how will I get to the railway station? Nor do I see any means of how I shall even cross the ferry wharf."

Daroga Babu replied, "Sharat Babu, please don't worry. I have arranged for a stretcher from the tea garden. I will send a few coolies to take you in it. One of my policemen would accompany you and wouldn't come back until you have boarded the train."

"Very well," I replied with my consent.

After receiving my consent, the two of them went away. It was about nine o'clock in the morning and I asked Digambar to fetch me a bowl of warm water. I wanted to sponge my body to freshen up a bit. Then, I had some barley. A few hours later, I even had some rice for lunch.

After noon, the men arrived with the stretcher to carry me. By that time, Revati Babu and Daroga Babu had already reached my house. Digambar and I were inside, busy packing my belongings when the fever struck again. Its assault was lethal, and my entire body was instantly engulfed by the bouts of shivering. I was unable to sit there even for a moment. So, I staggered back to my bedroom, unpacked the bedding, and fell on it. Before I could realize anything further, I fainted. Then, my whole consciousness was shrouded behind the sheath of enormous darkness.

When I regained consciousness, I noticed two things. In the dark, outside the window, a branch of some tree was swaying in the wind. Second, my trunk and other baggage were kept by the wall near my feet while my umbrella was leaning at the corner of that wall.

In that half-conscious state, I wondered . . . *Did I board the train? But why is it so dark within the compartment? Why aren't there any passengers inside?*

Then, as the clouds started to clear from my mind, I remembered that before I could even sit on the stretcher, I was engulfed by that horrible fever which forced me to lie on my bed. My mind questioned once again . . . *Well, if I am still inside the house, then where is Digambar? Why didn't he ignite a lamp? Why did he leave everything in the dark? No! Something is wrong. Where am I?'*

I felt thirsty, very thirsty. I tried to raise my voice to call Digambar, but my voice choked. I tried for the second time, but once again, no sound came out of my throat. As I looked around, it seemed as if the moon had come up and a few faint rays of that moonlight were entering the room through the open window.

Quietly, I tried to see what was ahead. There was a gripping silence inside the entire room. Then, as I looked outside, I saw someone . . .

My heart skipped a beat as it shrieked at me from within my ribcage. "Who is that?" I asked.

Even today, after so many years, I feel shaky when I remember that eerie incident. In that dim moonlight, I saw a young girl. Her skin was dark, and she was pacing all around the house, as if she was revolving around it from outside. She had a small stick in her hand with which, it seemed she was circling the house. The sight left me drowned in its impenetrable mystery while I helplessly remained on the bed and witnessed the bizarre episode.

Twice, she went past the door. As she did , she knelt deliberately while passing by. The third time, she stood momentarily, lifted her head, and waved at me softly. Then, she whispered to me, *Have no more fears . . . I am confining the house within this circle. Nothing can cross it tonight . . . Go to sleep without any worries . . .*

I saw her just for those few moments and then she vanished. I couldn't hold my consciousness any longer and fainted again. Did I fall asleep, or did I faint? I couldn't decipher.

I don't know how long after I woke up. However, when I opened my eyes, that little girl was sitting next to me. She was probably not more than eighteen years old. In that semi-conscious state, I could comprehend that much. I noticed that she was sweating heavily, which left me astounded. Her entire face and body were wet with her own perspiration.

As I looked at her, she looked back at me and said in a sweet and affectionate voice . . . *Why did you wake up? Go back to sleep . . . Go . . . Don't be afraid . . . Go to sleep . . .*

There was a soft motherly warmth in that voice, which sounded like a lullaby, and made me fall asleep once again.

Before I fell asleep, my eyes fell upon that branch, which I had seen outside the window, and it seemed soaked in a soft silvery moonshine.

The next morning, when I woke up, I was completely fit. It felt as though I had fully recovered from all the illness and regained my strength. There was no sign of any pain in my entire body, even though I was still very weak. I couldn't even get up from my bed. After a few hours, I saw Digambar. He cautiously tiptoed inside the house and peeped from outside into my room.

He looked startled as I raised my voice to call him. The man stood there without uttering a single word as if he was thunderstruck. I raised my voice again and said, "Go and call Revati Babu."

With a strange and puzzled expression on his face, he went away quickly to obey my order. Then, after a while, a lot of people came together to see me. Revati Babu too was among them.

He looked at me with disbelief in his eyes and asked, "Sharat Babu, how are you feeling now?"

I replied, "I am feeling much better, and I feel hungry. I want to eat something."

Revati Babu ran out and said something to somebody. The man hurried away and then quickly came back with a bowl of barley. In hunger, I gobbled up the food, and regained a bit of strength after the nourishment. Soon, the doctor arrived, checked me, and said with a sigh that my fever had vanished.

For the next two days, I gradually moved toward total recovery. Later, the residents of Haldia told me what had happened on that fateful night.

That night, the people of Haldia had anticipated the worst. Such was my condition that they were sure that I wouldn't survive beyond the night. Without any ray of hope in sight, they left me alone in my room and went away. The doctor had said that the critical condition of my illness would take away my life within the span of a few hours. The people even arranged for my funeral the following morning. They had made all the arrangements for the people who would carry my body for cremation and had also arranged the wood for the pyre. Daroga Babu had appointed a constable, from the police station, who would send a telegraph to my family with the news of my sudden death.

*

Sharat Chakraborty concluded, "However, in that solitary, abandoned condition when I was on my deathbed, who was that mysterious girl who sat beside me throughout the night? Who was that strange girl who drew that circle of safety around my house and protected me? When everyone lost their hopes and abandoned me to die, she was the one who sat there and guarded me throughout the fateful night. But who was that girl? I don't have any answers to these questions."

Sharat Chakraborty looked around at us, and added, "You can say that I was hallucinating while I was in a state of trance due to my critical state. I shall not deny. You could also say that it was my own imagination during the comatose condition.. I can only say that, even if it was a dream or a hallucination, it was the most profound and sweet one. My eyes shall eternally remain soaked in the residue of that ethereal dream. It has left a colossal ray of hope in my heart and my life."

As he finished, it seemed his eyes were moist due to the turmoil of emotions within his heart.

Nitaipada broke the silence and asked softly, "How long did you stay in Haldia after you got cured?"

Sharat Chakraborty replied, "I stayed there till the government didn't transfer me to a new place. It was almost two more years."

Nitaipada asked, "Did you continue to live alone in that house at Haldia?"

"Digambar and I were the two sole residents of my house at Haldia," Sharat Chakraborty replied.

Nitaipada added, "After that night, did you ever see anything similar?"

"Never," replied Sharat Chakraborty.

"Did you ever fall sick again?" asked Nitaipada.

"Never," added Sharat Chakraborty with a smile.

The night was dark, and the monsoon showers were incessant. Amid that, the fireflies were dancing around the branches of the jasmine tree. The impact of the story left us speechless, and we sat silently inside the clubhouse.

Even Nitaipada chose not to ask any more questions. Considering the fragile condition of the weather, we requested Sharat Chakraborty to go back home.

Who was that little girl who came to protect Sharat Chakraborty?

Was she a messiah or a goddess?

Was she a supernatural being whose soul felt pity and protected Sharat that night?

***

The Uncanny
Barriers to Birja Hom

Years ago, I heard a bizarre story from Bhairav Chakraborty. At that time, I was a teacher at Kadarpore High School. Kadarpore was a village in the Khulna district. I had just graduated from college and had taken up the job of teacher at the school.

Bhairav Chakraborty was a pious and orthodox Brahmin, but he commanded huge respect among the villagers. He used to devote one-eighth of the day to performing his diurnal worship. Once every month, he used to perform the sacred *Yajna of Birja Hom*[23]. From the hour past noon, he used to fasten a fresh flower on his *tiki*[24] religiously. He always cooked his own meals, just like a devout Brahmin. He purposely abstained from keeping any disciples because, as per

---

[23] This fire ritual, or Hom, is known as the 'Viraja Hom' or Birja Hom in Bengali. 'Viraja' is a Sanskrit word that means pure.

[24] A lock of hair left on top or on the back of the shaven head of a male Hindu.

him, it was a sin for a Brahmin to take money from his disciples. Despite being a pandit in Sanskrit, Bhairav Chakraborty never taught at a school. He even disliked the idea of teaching at *Sanskrit Tol*[25]. He strongly believed that such employment mostly stole away a lion's share of a person's time to think about the government's pay raises or to flatter Tol inspectors for undue favors. Despite all his prejudices, Bhairav Chakraborty did attend to a couple of poor students whom he used to feed at his house and used to teach Sanskrit grammar.

That year, the monsoons were delayed. Throughout the humid days and nights, there was no respite from the intolerable discomfort. Each day passed in anticipation of a little rain, but the weather always played truant. The school had just reopened after the summer vacation, but the extremely hot and humid climate compelled the students to make an appeal to the school authorities to shift the school's timing to an earlier period in the morning. Then, one day, at around three o'clock in the afternoon, a few clouds of rain appeared near the northeastern horizon.

The school's headmaster was sitting inside his own chamber when Gopi Babu, the History teacher, rushed in and said in an excited voice, "Sir, it is cloudy! Finally . . ."

Murli Mukherjee, the notorious headmaster, interrupted and asked in a somber voice, "What is cloudy?"

At first, Gopi Babu was taken aback by the response. He fumbled and replied, "Well, sir, CLOUDS . . . as we all know it."

"Alright, but how does it matter?" asked Murli Mukherjee in an irritated tone.

"Sir, that means it will rain today." replied Gopi Babu, "Sir, isn't it wise to cancel the rest of the classes for today? I mean, many

---

[25] Tol, as called in Bihar and Bengal, was the center of higher education. Some famous centers for Sanskrit education were Kasi (Varanasi), Tirhut (Mithila), Nadia, and Utkala.

students have come from far away and most of them haven't even brought their umbrellas."

"It won't rain today. Those are not rain clouds," interrupted Murli Mukherjee with sheer rudeness.

Perhaps even the chief clerk at the office of Lord Indra, the God of Rain, would've hesitated to make such an overconfident statement, but Murli Mukherjee considered himself far more adept in his forecast. Everyone in the school was aware of Murli Mukherjee's vast erudition in almost every subject. Forecasting weather conditions was like a child's play for him.

Gopi Babu lost his cheerful spirit and asked, "Will it not?"

"No," came the short and stout response.

"Why sir? There are a few rain clouds in the sky. Then, why won't it rain?" Gopi Babu asked helplessly.

"What do you understand about rain clouds? How much do you know about them?" asked Murli Mukherjee in a strong voice, "Those are cirrostratus clouds that do not carry rain."

I was resting inside the staffroom. Through the open window, the sight of the gathering clouds and the hope of a downpour made me feel delighted. I heard Murli Mukherjee's loud verdict and quickly came out to say, "But sir, even I think that it will rain today."

Murli Mukherjee replied with his usual stubbornness, "It doesn't mean that every cloud would cause a downpour. Remember, cirrostratus clouds do not produce precipitation."

I asked, "Then, which kind of cloud produces rain?"

Murli Mukherjee replied, "At this time, we need altostratus clouds for that. They are also known as sheet clouds."

"Okay," was the only reply I could give.

"Moreover, the wind is blowing from the south. Before the monsoons, it will turn toward the east," added Murli Mukherjee.

We didn't have the courage to argue with him further and chose not to speak anymore. But contrastingly, Lord Indra chose to shatter the pride of the haughty and boastful Murli Mukherjee! Within fifteen minutes, dark clouds gathered across the entire sky and then darker clouds covered them further. Then, just before the school's dismissal came the last stroke of Lord Indra with a bounty of incessant downpours. For the next two hours, the relentless showers played ruckus across the lands, overflowed every possible waterbody—including ponds, pits, and puddles—and finally came to a culmination at around five-thirty in the evening. As a result, all the students and the teaching staff were stuck inside the school until the rain receded.

Gopi Babu went to Murli Mukherjee and said in a victorious ecstasy, "See sir, didn't I tell you that it will rain today? We could have saved all the troubles if you would have listened to me and dismissed the classes earlier."

Murli Mukherjee replied with a frown, "Sometimes unpredictable things happen like that. You are a teacher of History, so you won't understand. You would've understood what I meant if you were a teacher of Mathematics! Across the universe, many strange and unpredictable things happen across time and space. Read Edward Garnet's article in this year's *Mathematical Gazette*. Understood?"

"What is that?" asked Gopi Babu with a puzzled face.

"I hope you have read *Alice in Wonderland*?" added Murli Mukherjee. "In Mathematics, it is like the experiment that is like *Alice Through the Looking Glass*! Read it and then you shall know."

Gopi Babu went away quickly. Discussions over Mathematics always made him diffident. As the showers stopped completely, Gopi Babu and I came out of the school. Within our hearts, both of us were happy. Fate had taught the arrogant headmaster a good lesson.

Suddenly, we saw Bhairav Chakraborty on the terrace in front of his house. He seemed extremely pleased about something. He saw us and said to me aloud, "How are you, Noni Babu? So, finally, it did rain. Right?"

"Oh yes Chakraborty Babu, Namaskar. Yes, it indeed happened," I replied.

"How could it not happen?" Bhairav Chakraborty replied with pride. "For the last three days, I have been continuously performing the sacred Hom so that it rains! How could those hours of my sacred ritual fail to bring the rain? It is impossible!"

"What are you saying? Is it so?" I replied, even though I didn't have any clue what to reply, "So, the downpours are the results of your sacred Hom."

Gopi Babu said in a murmur, "Well, all such claims are but strokes of good luck."

Bhairav Chakraborty could hear what he said. He said in a heavy voice, "Please come over. Let me show you."

Gopi Babu and I went up to the terrace and sat with him. There was a cheer in our hearts, and nothing seemed so bad. After days of discomfort due to the scorching and humid heat, the atmosphere had a soothing cool relief after the rains.

Soon, Bhairav Chakraborty took us inside the house. As we went in, we could see the arrangements. The fire was still simmering inside the pile of sand that was supposedly the *Yajna Kund*.[26] Adjacent to it, was a stack of dry wood. Beside it was the holy *Narayan Sheila*[27], which was on a copper plate, while containers of various sizes were filled with flowers and the holy *Belpatra*[28]. There was a small container with an ounce of sacred vermillion

---

[26] It is a reservoir in which sacred offerings of Hawan/Yajna Kund are kindled. It is a Vedic ritual in which people make a fire in the center and make offerings along with chantings of mantras to please a god/goddess and purify themselves and the environment around them.

[27] It is a revered stone worshipped by Vishnu Bhakts as Lord Narayana or Vishnu.

[28] Belpatra, also known as bael or Bengali quince, is a trifoliate leaf that signifies the three eyes of Lords Shiva, Brahma, and Vishnu.

too. The Yajna had been completed and it was evident from the things scattered all around.

Bhairav Chakraborty said, "Babu, now do you see it? Do you now see the effects of performing the sacred Hom?"

"Do you believe in the supernatural?" Gopi Babu asked Bhairav Chakraborty.

"Most definitely! I have witnessed it with my own eyes," replied Bhairav Chakraborty, "I have beheld so many ghastly apparitions while I sat on the *Panchamundi Asana*[29] during my sacred prayers."

Gopi Babu felt excited and asked, "Please tell us more about it. Or at the least, tell us one."

"No, let it be. I won't talk about those gruesome experiences," replied Bhairav Chakraborty, "but, less than a year ago, I experienced something at a host's house. It was truly supernatural. I will tell you about that incident. Before that, let me arrange for some tea."

Just then, the dark clouds gathered across the sky once again and a heavy downpour began. There was no way we could return home now. Everything became dark and a rainstorm started to unfurl with cold winds. There was no way we could even step out of Bhairav Chakraborty's house. The *Jam phal*[30] started to shower down it's abundance of fruits in his garden in that turmoil of Mother Nature. The frogs began to creak to welcome the delayed monsoon. So, we chose to stay back. It was useless to take shelter under our umbrellas in that heavy rainfall. Moreover, it gave us a golden opportunity to listen to Bhairav Chakraborty and his paranormal experiences while we sat on the mattress under the shade on his earthen terrace.

---

[29] It is ceremonial sitting spot as per Tantra Sadhana that is signified by 5 skulls (pancha mundi) with 4 in each corner and 1 in the center. The skulls can be of any animal with 1 mandatory human skull at the least.

[30] Java plum tree.

The tea arrived at the right time. Bhairav Chakraborty, while fetching some good quality tobacco, began narrating his story . . .

"Last year, during the month of Bhadra, one of my distant relatives informed me that one of his daughters was terribly sick. He pleaded with me to perform the auspicious yet difficult Birja Hom ritual to save the life of that little girl. It is believed that an impeccably performed Yajna is capable enough to save the life of a terminally ill patient too. Even I had heard about that miracle.

"They came and took me along. We sailed on a frail wooden boat across the tumultuous Yamuna River and then arrived at Gobardanga Station. As we reached their village, I saw that it was a distant rural place that was home to only a few Brahmin families. Most of the other residents were either families of milkmen or of uneducated wild and rural clans. The village was situated on the banks of the Yamuna River. It was so distant from civilization that in the absence of proper sanitation, the women bathed in the open waters of the river."

"What is the name of the village?" asked Gopi Babu suddenly.

"It was called Sao-bere," replied Bhairav Chakraborty. "The place was surrounded by dense and wild woods. In the entire village, there was only one small brick-built dilapidated temple of Lord Shiva. In the absence of proper supervision, overgrowth of *peepal* [31] and banyan had grown atop that ramshackle structure. I noticed that there was a huge *Shiv Linga* [32] inside the temple. That too was in a state of sheer state of neglect. It had been many years since anyone had worshipped the idol inside that abandoned temple."

At this moment, Bhairav Chakraborty's eldest daughter, Shaila, brought us some refreshments. Her father was a widower and she

---

[31] Also known as sacred fig, it is considered to have religious importance in the Indian subcontinent.

[32] A symbol that represents Lord Shiva in Hinduism.

had come down from her husband's place to be with him for a couple of days.

Then, Bhairav Chakraborty continued, "Remember this temple of Lord Shiva. It has a subtle connection to the story.

"As we reached our destination, I freshened up. The host then took me inside a room. The sick girl was lying on the bed. She was probably thirteen or fourteen years old. Around her neck, I could see a cluster of amulets. With her eyes closed, her body was turned on one side, but she wasn't asleep. As I walked in, she lifted her head and looked at me.

"She had a fever, and that too was very high. The temperature was around 103 degrees. Her eyes were tired due to exhaustion, and the corners of her eyes were red. I sat down and checked her pulse. It was decently strong. I didn't observe any immediate signs of danger. Moreover, I was not there for her treatment. I was there to perform the Birja Hom for her.

"The girl's father, Mohan, said, 'Please bless us! You are a holy man, and we are blessed by your presence in our house.'

"Just as I had raised my hand to bless him, to my sheer surprise, Mohan slipped and fell on the floor with a bang. The floor was dry and there was no reason for anyone to slip and fall. It was beyond all explanation. My hand trembled and the others rushed in to help Mohan.

"How did he fall? Nobody could understand. Hence, my blessings remained ungiven. Mohan's brother-in-law came to his aide and treated his wounds with cold water. The little girl started to weep. Within those few moments, everything had gone into chaos.

"A sudden remorse gripped my heart. I am a tantric and I engage in various rituals and religious practices. I have the power to sense such indications. That day, all the indications hinted toward something ominous.

"Should I then not perform the Birja Hom? The question started to haunt me.

"The climate was humid and inside the house, there was a complete absence of fresh air; it felt suffocating. As evening fell, I went out and strolled across the little road in front of the temple of Lord Shiva. Despite the humid climate, there was some fresh air in the open.

"Suddenly, I heard a whisper . . . 'Listen . . . Listen to me.'

"Twice, the voice called me. I was puzzled by the suddenness and looked here and there. Then, I noticed something in the dark. Near the doorsteps of the temple, there stood a shadowy feminine figure.

"I looked at her and asked, 'Are you calling me?'

"The shadowy figure whispered back in a disturbing voice, 'Don't perform the Birja Hom. That girl is destined to die! She will not live . . .'

"'Who are you?' I asked.

"'I might be anybody, but that is not of any concern,' she replied, 'it is for your greater good that you listen to my words. I forbid you to perform the Birja Hom.'

"I was very astonished. In that dark evening, how did a woman suddenly come up in front of the dilapidated temple? Honestly, I felt somewhat angry too. Who was she to forbid me? I was a holy man, and I didn't care about ghosts and apparitions. She was a mere rustic woman and how could she dare to command me? With the blessings of the Divine Mother, everything was possible. I, Bhairav Chakraborty, was desperate to hold on to my decisions and didn't fear anybody.

"I went back to the house but didn't tell anyone about the shadowy woman and her warning. I sat down with Mohan and made a list of the items that were needed to perform the Birja Hom. At around eight o' clock, I got up to prepare my dinner.

"However, before coming to it, let me give you a brief idea about the house. It was an old brick-built house that didn't possess any architectural beauty, but it was a two-storied one. The house was not located right on the banks of the Yamuna River. It was a little far away from it. In between, there was just one house. Between the two houses, there was a gap of about ten or twelve feet.

"There was a small room on the rooftop, which was given to me. On the adjacent open roof, arrangements were made so that I could cook my dinner in an earthen oven. I was alone on the rooftop and was busy cooking a simple meal of boiled rice, pulses, and potatoes, and I planned to have them with some ghee. By the time I finished cooking, it was quite late in the night. A thick blanket of darkness had almost covered everything around me. I smoked a bit of tobacco to rest for some time and then sat down to eat my dinner. However, as soon as I sat, I could sense that I was not alone on that roof. It was an uncanny feeling that gripped my consciousness, and I looked around everywhere. The eerie sense didn't vanish, even though I failed to find anybody else on the roof. It was indeed strange. The people of that household had long gone to sleep and at that late hour, the entire village was asleep too. Only the faint and distant sounds of the fishermen, on their fishing boats that were afloat on the Yamuna, could be heard.

"I tried to divert my mind and began to eat. Suddenly, I lifted my head and froze.

"My heart questioned my mind . . . *What is that tall and dark figure in front of me? Is it a tree? I had been cooking on the rooftop for so long, so why didn't I notice it earlier? Maybe it was there, and I didn't notice it, or else how am I able to see it now? But . . . what tree is that? Well . . . before I started to cook, I could clearly see a bullock cart pass in between the two houses. No . . . even then I didn't see this tall tree . . .'*

"*Is it a palm tree? No, but what sort of palm tree is that?*' my mind shrieked in horror as I left my meal, jumped, and stood up.

"No, it wasn't a palm tree. Even today, when I think of that incident, it raises every hair on my body with fear.

"On the cornice of the roof's parapet, I saw a huge monstrous demon! It was a devilish apparition with a giant body and equally giant limbs. Its head was like a gigantic tumbler and its eyes were like two burning kilns of fire. With its glance fixed upon me, the demonic apparition was perhaps trying to turn me into ashes with the glare!

"The ghastly creature was huge. Tall as a palm tree, its head was high up in the sky, staring at me from above.

"I was speechless. I still couldn't believe what I was seeing with my eyes. I rubbed my eyes a couple of times and took a closer look. But no, it wasn't an illusion. The horrible creature was a real apparition that was standing in front of me like an enormous evil cluster of darkness. Moreover, beyond the roof's parapet and above it, I could only see its body partially. To be precise, from its belly to its head. The rest of its body was under the parapet because the creature wasn't standing on the roof; it was standing between the two houses!

"Within those few moments, I looked at that horrific creature multiple times and was yet unable to move a step. I can vouch that if anybody else would've seen that creature that night, then that person would've certainly died out of fear.

"Believe me, I have seen many ghastly creatures. When one sits on the Panchamundi Asana, they come to haunt you and disrupt your ritual just before you are about to complete it. Yet, none of those could even match that gigantic monster!

"I was gripped by an unimaginable terror while my body shook in fear. I felt I would faint.

"As I struggled to control my senses, I started to chant the

Taara Mantra[33]. I raised my voice, stared at the devilish monster, and chanted it as loud as I could. Soon, the creature vanished into thin air. Once again, I rubbed my eyes and took a closer look. The creature was gone.

"Alarmingly, as soon as it vanished, from downstairs, came loud wails of despair. The family was weeping aloud. Their little girl had died.

"It happened almost instantaneously. How was it possible? I could never find the reason. I just revealed the facts that had unfolded in front of my eyes and whatever I had experienced personally. Now, it is up to you to believe me or not."

*

The story was intriguing, and it left both Gopi Babu and me speechless. No, we didn't doubt Bhairav Chakraborty. Neither could we find any explanation behind whatever had happened.

It was true that Bhairav Chakraborty failed to perform the Birja Hom which could've saved the girl. However . . .

Why did that shadowy woman forbid him to perform it? Why were the words of caution whispered?

Why was Bhairav Chakraborty stopped from performing the Birja Hom?

Was it the incarnate of 'death' himself?

***

---

[33] The holy chants for goddess Kali (another name of her is Taara).

The Devil's Teacup

It was a simple and mundane thing. An enamel teacup and saucer that was worth of hardly three *anna*[34]. I still remember the day when it first came into our household many years ago. It was a lazy winter afternoon. I had just finished my lunch and was preparing to get inside the quilt on my cozy bed for a quick nap, when the voice of my Kaka, my father's younger brother, reached my ears and dragged me out to the terrace. I knew that he had gone to the mela at the Koolbere Village and the cheer in his voice clearly suggested that he had done a decent business at the place.

Two bullock carts were being offloaded in the courtyard. Hari Maity, the farmer, was taking down a bundle of new mattresses. There was a large basket containing various household items, like new utensils, floor mats, two new stools made of jackfruit wood, a heap of spinach stems, two barrels of date palm jaggery, and many more goodies that were unloaded from it.

---

[34] A former monetary unit of India, equal to one-sixteenth of a rupee.

Kaka saw me and said, "Niru, go and fetch a lantern. This one doesn't have any oil."

Niru was the nickname for Nirupam.

I ran inside and got a lantern from the kitchen. *Pishima*[35] howled at me for the act.

I went back and asked Kaka, "How was the crowd at the mela this time?"

He replied, "At first, the crowd was decent in number and business was good too. But suddenly, an assault of cholera came as an unexpected nemesis. As people started to die—about four or five deaths happened every day—the others began to flee. Then, the police arrived and shut down the mela. All the eateries were forced to shut down too. Even then, the situation didn't improve. At last, with no hope of improvement, we too ran away and came home. Hopefully, whatever I have earned will cover the expenses and wages incurred on the trip."

As we sat down for dinner, Kaka talked about his experience at the mela while the rest of the family sat and listened to him. It was a horrid tale of his equally horrible experience with the assault of the deathly cholera and the deaths of so many innocent people.

Kaka said, "A pious Brahmin named Jadu Chakraborty had come to visit the mela with his entire family. They had parked their bullock cart under a large tree by the riverbank. Two days later, they were supposed to return. Unfortunately, before that could happen, the horrible cholera struck the entire place! At first, their nine-year-old daughter was infected. With the absence of doctors and medicines, the little girl passed away the next morning. But that was not the end of their ordeal. Soon after, her mother was afflicted and she too passed away. Next were Jadu Chakraborty's son and daughter-in-law! Ah, the poor Brahmin's family was finished within days."

---

[35] In Bengali, Pishima is one's father's sister.

Kaka was a trader of grains. He had taken along forty maund of *moong dal*[36] to the mela, but he could hardly manage to sell twelve or thirteen maund. Bullock carts full of the remaining stock were to arrive back soon.

Kaka finished his meal and went away. Soon, his little daughter, Manu, came with an enamel teacup and saucer set. She showed it to my mother and said excitedly, "See, Baba has got this for three anna from the mela. Tomorrow, I will drink tea in this teacup. Look, isn't it beautiful? I just saw it."

Time moved on and eight years went by. As I grew up, I started a business of tube wells. It was a prosperous business and I had learned and mastered the skills. I collected most of my orders from the State and District Boards of the Government. My work made me travel extensively and I seldom stayed at home.

One evening, I was supposed to return to Calcutta by the night's train. I had finished my packing and had asked for some tea. As I went near the kitchen, I heard my niece Manu say, "Pishima, don't give tea to anyone in that teacup. After Baba's demise, Maa cannot even stand a glance of that thing."

I went inside and asked, "Which teacup are you talking about? What happened with it?"

My niece went and fetched the teacup. I saw it and recalled that it was the same enamel teacup that, many years ago, Kaka had brought from the mela.

She said in a somber voice, "When your cousin sister-in-law was sick, she used to drink milk from that teacup. Even Baba used to have his barley from the same teacup. That is why Maa cannot tolerate it."

Indeed, a distant cousin and his wife had come to visit us. But his wife suddenly fell ill and died. Two years later, Kaka got sick and

---

[36] It refers to split and skinned mung beans, known as petite yellow lentils.

passed away. However, what was the relation of that teacup with the two deaths? It was a mere superstition.

The following year, my business grew further in prosperity. I got engrossed in extensive travel across the districts to appoint laborers and complete the assignments. The remaining time went into collecting previous payments. As I became busier, a shroud of domestic quarrels covered the family. Until Kaka was alive, there was a discipline in the family that nobody dared to challenge. After his demise, everyone wanted to become their own masters.

Then one day, my younger son suddenly fell ill. I was away in the districts and the subdivisions, finishing pending works and unearthing payments, which would otherwise get delayed for months. Alas, by the time I reached home, my little child was gone! It was an unexpected shock that shook me to the core.

By the end of the same year, I took my wife and children and relocated to the city. After that horrible incident, nobody wanted to stay in the village. So, I took them along and settled in the city.

As I became more mature professionally, I realized a fact that is true even to this day. The rural population of Bengal is extremely lazy, and such is the extent of their lethargy that they even defy the onslaught of imminent death and gulp it down as a granted fact. I wondered about how every villager in rural Bengal could be so indifferent about their own wellbeing and remain satisfied with the most minimal resources? How could they continue to endure hardships and pangs of poverty but won't step out to resolve the issues? Maybe my extensive travels, which my business imposed upon me, had changed my perspective. Otherwise, who knows, even I would've been just like them! However, these people have one capability. They never complain about anything. Not about the country, neither about the government, nor about the almighty! They are even satisfied with what destiny has provided them. A stranger would call them dead or non-living. No, trust me, they are not dead.

From the outside, their inertia might seem to be lifeless, but a closer look would definitely prove otherwise. They aren't dead. Perhaps, they would never even be so. They have an uncanny and endless vitality that prevents them from dying! Such is the strangeness of that vigor that they continue to struggle with death, and get defeated continually at every step, but they don't become dispirited or get crushed by fear. So, in that colossal lethargy, in every situation, they refrain from taking any action to prevent their misfortunes too! Hence, despite the onslaughts of cholera from the contaminated waters of the ponds and pits, they would never even take the step to install a tube well to get hygienic drinking water. It was and still is, like a mammoth responsibility that no one wanted to undertake.

One evening, I noticed that my youngest niece was drinking tea from that enameled teacup. Even though I wasn't a superstitious person, an unknown uneasiness gripped me from inside. After we finished having our tea, I sneaked inside the kitchen, took out that teacup and saucer and went out into the veranda. Then, drawn by some unknown force, I threw it out, beyond the boundary of my house, into an adjacent cluster of woods.

Little Mithu was ten years old, and she was the youngest daughter of my Kaka. She was a witty and intelligent child. After I had moved my family to the city, I had brought her along from the village. Kaka was no more and her elder sister, Manu, too had been married. I used to admire the child and wanted to provide her with a proper education in the city.

Six months passed and it was the month of Baisakh. Suddenly, I got overwhelmed with work. With orders for tube well installations across the districts, I had to run around without a moment of relief. I could hardly stay at home with my family as every tour would last for almost ten days! The relentless burden of touring earned me money, but I was losing the opportunity to spend some golden moments with my children.

One day, a letter arrived. Mithu was severely ill. In sheer horror, I rushed back home. It was a few hours past noon when I reached home. As I entered the patient's room, I was left thunderstruck by the sight in front of me! Pishi Maa was feeding Mithu some barley. And she was doing so from that enameled teacup!

At that moment, my subconscious mind could only think of it as the . . . *DEVIL'S TEACUP!*

I took my daughter aside and said in a scared voice, "Where did you get that teacup from?"

She replied, "A stray dog or a cat had probably taken it away into the adjacent woods beyond our house's boundary wall. Didi found it and got it back. Baba, that was long ago."

I was astonished and asked her, "She got it? Are you sure about it?"

She looked at me blankly for some time and then replied, "Yes, I am very sure about it. If you don't believe me then you can ask Maa. Remember that young servant who was bitten by a dog? On that same day, Didi got it back from the woods. And it was the same teacup from which the servant was fed some herbal decoction!"

My voice trembled as I asked, "Are you talking about Ram Lagan?"

"Yes Baba," my daughter replied, "after that incident, he returned to his village."

My entire body began to shiver. Everyone knew that Ram Lagan had returned home. However, I had never revealed to anybody that soon after he went back, the poor chap died.

Till that time, Mithu was not so ill. The doctor said that there was nothing to fear, and that she would recover shortly. However, the shrieks of an evil shadow kept echoing within my heart.

Nobody else knew about the dark history of that teacup. By then, I knew that it was like the devil's chalice. Any sick person who drank or ate something from that teacup had most definitely died. It was the harbinger of death and had the power to snatch away life! This was a fact that only my eldest daughter and I knew. But, despite all the strangeness, it was true.

A while later, I stole the cursed teacup and saucer again from the kitchen. I didn't want anyone else to panic. But the moment I touched it, shivers ran down my spine! The touch was so very alive! It was as if I had touched the body of a venomous snake whose one bite was potent enough to end any human being's life. That lethal coldness in its ghostly touch had a ruthless, cruel, and villainous vibe to it. In every breath, that venomous monster was breathing out the airs of death.

Then, the inevitable happened. The devil's verdict was too strong to be defied.

The next morning, Mithu's condition started to worsen . . . Then, on the ninth day, our dear Mithu passed away.

What was the curse hidden in the teacup? Why did it refuse to go away? From where did it come into the mortal world? Was it truly the devil's teacup?

I could never find the answers . . .

***

About the Author

Bibhutibhushan Bandyopadhyay (September 12, 1894–November 1, 1950) was one of the pioneers of Bengali literature who is best known for his works like *Pather Panchali*, *Aparajito*, *Chander Pahar*, and *Aranyak*. He is a stalwart in his way of expressing his views about the world, society, and the bounty of Mother Nature.

Apart from being a teacher, he traveled extensively across Bengal while working different jobs. While traversing through the forests of Chota Nagpur, Hazaribagh, Ranchi, and Manbhum, he garnered vast experiences, which were subsequently incorporated into his stories. Set mainly in rural Bengal, his stories encompass the landscape and lifestyle of that era with vivid descriptions and elaborate dialogue that bring the characters to life.

Bibhutibhushan's writings not only express his deep understanding of the people of rural Bengal through their hardships, sufferings, hopes and dreams, but they also come out as expressions of human triumph in the face of adversities. Bibhutibhushan was a passionate lover of nature and its abundant beauty across Bengal. Almost all his works are decorated with vivid descriptions of the enthralling beauty he could see in the wilderness. He was an avid reader who deeply understood every subject he had covered in his stories. Even as one looks into his works of horror, paranormal or the occult, one can feel the depth of his knowledge. He had penned down the narratives in his simple language so that his readers could taste the flavors of his stories.

Born in Muratipur Village, near Kalyani in Nadia, at his maternal uncle's house, Bibhutibhushan spent his early years in his home at Barrackpore, West Bengal. In 1921, Bibhutibhushan published his first short story, *Upekshita*, in the leading Bengali magazine, *Probashi*. However, his literary talent received critical acclaim only when his first novel, *Pather Panchali* (i.e., Song of the Little Road), was published while he stayed at Ghatshila, a town in Jharkhand. It was initially released as a serial in a periodical in 1928 and then as a book in 1929. This work and its sequel, *Aparajito,* brought Bandyopadhyay to the limelight in Bengali literature and were subsequently translated into numerous languages.

Many of Bibhutibhushan's epic works were adapted into movies, too. Satyajit Ray adapted *Pather Panchali* in 1955 and created the *Apu Trilogy* (*Pather Panchali, Aparajito, and Apur Sansar*). This work is still considered one of the classics of world cinema. Bibhutibhushan's created character, Apu, had been immortalized by Ray in this epic trilogy. Ray even adapted the critically acclaimed work of Bibhutibhushan, titled *Ashani Sanket*. Many of these cinematic adaptations went on to win several national and international awards.

At the age of fifty six years, Bibhutibhushan passed away on 1st November 1950 in Ghatshila. In 1951, the most prestigious literary award in West Bengal, Rabindra Puraskar, was posthumously awarded to Bibhutibhushan for his novel *Ichamati*.

About the Translator

Prasun Roy is the author of several bestselling books known for their gripping and appealing narrative style written in simple language. His written works encompass various genres, including biography, translations, history, mythology, and the paranormal. Prasun has a remarkable lineup of fiction titles in various mystery, adventure, young adult, and thriller subgenres. Two of his fiction titles have been selected as supplementary reads for students at a prominent school in Vadodara.

Prasun has delivered lectures at eminent institutes like IIT Kanpur; Maharaja Sayajirao University (Baroda); IIT Delhi in association with IHAR, DRDO, Ministry of Culture, Ministry of Defense, IGNCA, Rishihood University; All India Radio, and The National Library. He has been a prominent speaker at many prestigious literary festivals, including Tata Steel Kolkata Literary Meet, Valley of Words International Literature & Arts Festival (Dehradun), Ahmedabad International Literature Festival, and Pune International Literary Festival.

Prasun lives with his family in Kolkata. An alumnus of IIM Lucknow and La Martiniere for Boys and Dolna Day School, he runs his family-owned pharmaceutical manufacturing and marketing business jointly headquartered in Vadodara and Kolkata.

More from Fingerprint's Horror Library

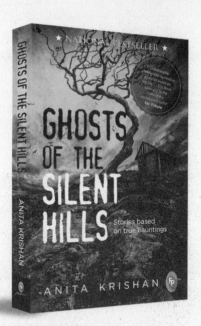

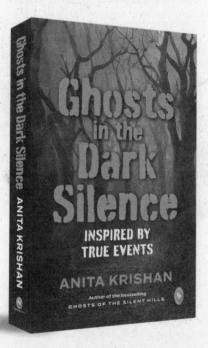